THE SHADOW OF THE MAMMOTH

Also by Fabio Morábito

Home Reading Service
Mothers and Dogs

THE SHADOW OF THE MAMMOTH

STORIES

FABIO MORÁBITO

Translated from the Spanish by Curtis Bauer

Other Press | New York

Stories in this collection originally published in Spanish as
La sombra del mamut in 2022 by Sexto Piso, Mexico City
Copyright © 2022 Fabio Morábito
Translation copyright © 2025 Curtis Bauer

Production editor: Yvonne E. Cárdenas
Text designer: Patrice Sheridan
This book was set in Adobe Janson Pro by
Alpha Design & Composition of Pittsfield, NH

1 3 5 7 9 10 8 6 4 2

All rights reserved. No part of this publication may be reproduced or transmitted in any form or by any means, electronic or mechanical, including photocopying, recording, or by any information storage and retrieval system, without written permission from Other Press LLC, except in the case of brief quotations in reviews for inclusion in a magazine, newspaper, or broadcast. Printed in the United States of America on acid-free paper. For information write to Other Press LLC, 267 Fifth Avenue, 6th Floor, New York, NY 10016. Or visit our Web site: www.otherpress.com

Library of Congress Cataloging-in-Publication Data
Names: Morábito, Fabio, 1955- author. | Bauer, Curtis, 1970- translator.
Title: The shadow of the mammoth : stories / Fabio Morábito ;
translated from the Spanish by Curtis Bauer.
Other titles: Sombra del mamut. English
Description: New York : Other Press, 2025.
Identifiers: LCCN 2025004337 (print) | LCCN 2025004338 (ebook) |
ISBN 9781635425321 (paperback) | ISBN 9781635425338 (ebook)
Subjects: LCGFT: Short stories.
Classification: LCC PQ7298.23.O724 S6613 2025 (print) |
LCC PQ7298.23.O724 (ebook) | DDC 863/.64—dc23/eng/20250310
LC record available at https://lccn.loc.gov/2025004337
LC ebook record available at https://lccn.loc.gov/2025004338

Publisher's Note: This is a work of fiction. Names, characters, places, and incidents either are the product of the author's imagination or are used fictitiously, and any resemblance to actual persons, living or dead, events, or locales is entirely coincidental.

CONTENTS

The Nail in the Wall   1
The Great Floating Road   10
Landing on the Moon   18
Artemis and the Stag   27
The Grass at Airports   41
Slow Dance   47
The Entertainer   57
Extras   72
Murder in the Gladiolus   80
Time to Take Out the Trash   91
Wildlife Crossing   101
The Sadness of Translation   110
Letters to the Queen   125
Daedalus Under Berlin   140
The Ravine   153
The Ball in the Water   164
The Mont Blanc Tunnel   181
The Shadow of the Mammoth   184

THE NAIL IN THE WALL

It was Sunday. Mónica wanted to hang a picture on the wall, a small Walter Lazzaro reproduction, and I didn't want to. The wall wasn't actually a wall, but one of the four square columns that delineate the perimeter of the room. It's a narrow column, but wide enough to hang a small picture on it. At first I'd agreed, went for the hammer and pounded a nail into the spot where we both thought it should hang. We really liked Lazzaro's painting: a fisherman's boat abandoned on the sand of the beach; there was nothing but the boat and turquoise sea stretching as far as the eye could see. Then someone knocked on the door. Mónica went to see who it was. It was one of our neighbors in the building, and she and Mónica started to talk about a discrepancy with the maintenance fees. I remembered a program I didn't want to miss, turned on the TV, and sat down to watch it. Mónica had to go downstairs with the neighbor to talk to the person in charge of collecting the building fees, and Lazzaro's painting was momentarily forgotten on one of the dining room chairs. The column was directly in front of where I was sitting, right behind the TV, and I noticed the nail. It caught my attention because it was right where it needed to be, in the middle of the column. Without using the tape measure, just by eyeing it, we had found its center, in relation not only to the width but also to the height. Well, this isn't entirely accurate. The nail was near the top of the column, in that area closest to the ceiling where paintings are usually hung. However, in relation to the whole column, it was as if we had found its true center, or rather its heart, and there was something magical about that. It was, so to speak, the ideal spot for a painting, so ideal that we didn't have to hang anything up anymore. The nail was an excellent substitute for any painting.

When Mónica returned, seeing the Lazzaro painting still on the chair, she asked why I hadn't hung it up and I asked her to sit next to me. I grabbed her hand. Mónica's hands are always cold, it could be something hereditary, and when she was sitting down I told her to look at the nail.

"What's wrong with it?" she asked.

"Don't you see it? It's perfect," I said.

"What are you talking about?"

"The nail."

She laughed.

"Don't be stupid," she said, getting up.

"I'm not joking," I told her. "We've never set a nail so perfectly and the painting's going to ruin it."

She realized that I was serious.

"What are you talking about?"

"You're not looking at it the right way. We identified and then placed the nail on the best part of the column. We don't have to put anything else there. It looks beautiful the way it is." She ignored me and grabbed Lazzaro's painting so she could hang it on the nail.

"No!" I shouted, grabbing it out of her hands.

Mónica looked at me as if I'd slapped her.

"What's wrong with you? Have you lost your mind?"

I thought that if she hung it, everything would go to hell. Once covered by a painting, the nail would lose its power, so to speak. I tried to explain that to her, but she looked at me in that way that made my guts churn:

"If you aren't going to hang that painting you're going to take this fucking nail out of the wall," and she went into the kitchen and slammed the door. I, having stood up, sat back down, leaving the painting where it was.

It was Sunday, like I said. The worst day for a fight. Later I tried to smooth things out when I asked her if she wanted some tequila. On Saturdays and Sundays Mónica and I have tequila before lunch. Her response was a simple no. I poured one for myself and went back to sit in front of the TV, leaving the Lazzaro painting on the chair.

I kept looking at the nail, and every time I looked at it, I had a very clear sense that we shouldn't hang anything there; that the nail was the painting. It wasn't bothering anyone, it was just a black dot on the column and it produced a sense of fairness, transcendence, and order. Something like an altar. A secular altar, without crucifixes or devotional images. A connection to the cosmos. Every house should have that, a connection to the cosmos, some way out from inside its walls, the walls that protect you, yes, but they also suffocate you.

It was a difficult Sunday. By the time I went to bed I was exhausted from the effort to avoid crossing paths with Mónica as much as possible in our minuscule apartment.

The next day when she left for the office, we said goodbye with a lukewarm farewell, a sign less of reconciliation than of weariness from having systematically eluded each other during the previous day.

Paulina arrived at her usual time. She started dusting with her cloth and I told her I wanted to point something out to her; I showed her the nail and told her not to remove it for any reason. Paulina is a brusque woman and sometimes she throws away the things she thinks are useless.

"Of course not, señor. Are you going to hang a picture?"

"No, I'm going to leave the pristine nail where it is, that's why I asked you to look at it, so you don't think about removing it."

"Do you want me to dust it?" And she raised her hand to wipe it off.

"No, no, leave it like it is."

I regretted showing it to her. Now the nail had become something important for her, something to be treated with great care, like my books, and the last thing I wanted was to cast that corner of the apartment in a halo of particular importance.

That night and the following nights, when I sat with Mónica to watch TV, I couldn't stop looking at the nail out of the corner of my eye, trying to hide it from her, because she'd certainly get angry. Indeed, she noticed.

"Do you have to keep looking at it all the time?" she said.

"What?"

"You know what."

"Does it bother you?"

"Yes. At least when you're with me, you could stop looking at it."

"If Lazzaro's painting were hanging there you wouldn't mind if I looked at it."

"Because a painting is a painting and it's painted to be looked at, but who would think of looking at a nail?"

"I like it."

"Well, I hate it!" she exclaimed. "Do you think it's fun to sit in front of the TV while you stare at a nail on the wall?"

"If I looked at it all the time I'd agree with you, but I only look at it from time to time. Are you going to tell me what I can and can't look at now?"

She threw the piece of fabric she was holding to the floor and looked at me angrily.

"Okay, since you like nails so much now, I'm going to give you something else to enjoy." She stood up, walked to the back wall, and began to remove each of the paintings, one by one.

"What are you doing?"

"You're looking at it: I'm removing the paintings so you can feast your eyes on all the nails."

"Mónica," I said, trying not to raise my voice, "don't be stupid."

She didn't answer me. She removed the paintings from the wall, did the same with the wall next to it, and ended up taking down all the paintings in the room.

"There," she said, "now you can enjoy the view at your leisure."

Mónica and I sleep in separate rooms because she can't stand my snoring. I turned off the TV, got up from the sofa, and went to my room. I started to read, but I was listening for her movements. A while later I heard the TV come on again. I kept reading until I fell asleep.

The next day, after waking up, I went to the kitchen to make myself a cup of coffee. The paintings were on the living room floor, leaning against one of the walls, and you could see the mark each one had left on the other walls.

With the characteristic maneuvering of couples who have been fighting for years, we managed to avoid even the slightest contact until she left for work. My schedule is more flexible than hers, so it's usually up to me to wait for Paulina to arrive. Mónica had left a message for her in the kitchen asking her to spend the morning cleaning off the marks the paintings had left on the living room walls.

Paulina set herself to the task right away. I was getting ready to leave when she called me over to ask if she also had to clean where the nail was on the column.

"No, Paulina, we haven't hung anything there," I told her.

"That's what it looks like, it's very clean."

"Yes, leave that one as it is."

It was the second time I'd told her to leave it as it was. I wondered what Paulina thought of that useless nail. Perhaps, with the fatalism typical of people like her, she had concluded without any major issues that in spite of all my books, or rather because of them, I was a little off in the head, which must have given her some pleasure, because it reduced the distance that separated us.

As I rode the elevator down I wondered if Paulina wasn't right. I was a little out of my mind, because who would put a nail in the wall to hang a picture and, after looking at the nail, decide that it looks better without it? What would the Louvre or the Prado be like if they applied the same principle? Excuse me, sir, I can't find *La Gioconda*, can you tell me where it is? My apologies, sir, after putting the nail in we saw that the wall looked better with nothing, so we have stored *La Gioconda* in the basement.

By the time I returned at noon, Paulina was gone. The marks from the paintings in the living room had disappeared. Without them, the nails, without any connection to each other, looked like crushed insects.

Paulina had left a message for me on the living room cabinet telling me that my wife had called to ask me to hang the paintings in their places. I was hungry and went to heat up my lunch. As I ate, I kept looking at the bare walls. Without the paintings, the room had the untidy air of being moved into or out of. I remembered what had happened to a friend when he moved. He was so engrossed in packing up the furniture, rugs, books, and other household items that he forgot to take his paintings. He told me that when he was leaving the apartment and took a last look to see if anything was left behind, the paintings were there, hanging right in front of him, but he didn't see them, and he attributed it to the fact that, after looking at them for so long, they had all become part of the walls, like the crown moldings and baseboards, which are things no one takes with them when they move out.

I finished my lunch and started to hang them back up. Gradually the walls came back to life. But my doubts began to creep back in. With the larger ones there was no way I could go wrong, but with some of the midsize and smaller ones I wasn't quite sure where we'd hung them. I had always bragged about my photographic memory and now realized it wasn't that good. I started trying various combinations to jog my memory about which one went where. I thought it would take me ten or fifteen minutes to hang the paintings, and an hour later I was still there, standing in front of the first wall. I was about to throw in the towel and wait for Mónica to come back. She had taken them down, so now she could put them back. But I thought that if I gave up, I'd be saying she was right, that she had won our little quarrel, because it would demonstrate that her relationship with the paintings was more intimate than mine and that my determination to leave the nail on the column in plain sight was just a whim on my part. So I didn't give up and continued with my task. After two hours, more because I was tired than out of conviction, I finished hanging them up. And then, as I looked at the bare column, with its nail in plain sight, its magical attraction suddenly ceased, as if hanging all the paintings had put an end to the raison d'être of that single empty space. Standing in front of it, I now saw only a nail thirsty for a painting, like all the others. I resisted at first, but finally went over to the small Lazzaro reproduction. When I hung it I felt my insides turning. It looked spectacular. It seemed to have been painted for that exact spot. I was overwhelmed with profound sadness and I had a premonition that something was gone forever. Something, I don't know what. That night, sitting in front of the TV, I kept glancing at the lonely boat out of the corner of my eye, at the turquoise sea in the background, and Mónica, of course, noticed. "It's beautiful, isn't it," she said, and with her cold hand she squeezed mine.

THE GREAT FLOATING ROAD

There's nothing the Chinese can't do when a king commands it. They have the Great Wall, but that wasn't the only cyclopean structure that was erected in ancient China. Another was the Great Floating Road, almost unknown until recently because it is in a difficult-to-reach region, between treacherously high hills and deep gorges. The king of that mountainous country, tired of seeing so much poverty around him, asked the master builders of the court to create a road where he could contemplate the beautiful scenery without having to encounter any villagers. A king needs from time to time to forget about his people, he told them. The master builders studied the map of the region at length and came to the conclusion that the one road that would avoid all contact with people could only be a road that never touched the ground. It should also be long enough to provide the king the opportunity for a prolonged excursion and varied enough to soothe his mood. After spending months inspecting every inch of the region, they plotted a route on the map that, winding between the hills, crossing bridges, and entering long tunnels, would not for a single moment touch the plains where the people lived. In short, it would be a floating highway, made up of fifteen tunnels and more than forty bridges along which the king would pass from one to another, contemplating his region from above.

In view of the magnitude of the project, thousands of workers had to be employed, toiling day and night in exhausting shifts. Many of them died as a result of the cave-ins and collapses that occurred in the tunnels and on the bridges. The work eventually consumed all the able-bodied men from around the region, leaving only women, old men, and children on the plains. Agriculture was abandoned and only pastoralism survived. Across the plains people were dying of hunger, on the mountain slopes many workers died during the construction project, either by falling from the scaffolding or from simple exhaustion, and the king, who had started that enterprise as a young man, was middle-aged by the time he saw it finished. On the summer morning it was inaugurated, he rode along the Great Floating Road in his carriage, accompanied by the queen and the two highest-ranking members of his court. Behind, in another carriage, was the rest of his entourage. The bridges and tunnels had been built to the exact size of the royal carriage, not one centimeter wider, which would have meant an increase in material and labor. In this way, the road could be traveled only in one direction and, once the journey had begun, it was impossible to change one's mind and return, because there wasn't enough room to turn around. Only on one bridge midway along the road had the master builders planned an area wide enough to allow the carriages and horses to turn around; after that point, the traveler had no choice but to continue until he arrived back at the castle again, crossing over other hills and ravines. The workers were relieved of their duties and returned to the plains, the population began to grow again, crops reappeared, and the poverty from the years before once again dissipated across the region. Now, however, the king could observe it from afar, as he traveled along the Great Floating Road accompanied by the queen or by one of his mistresses. The villages were mere specks in the distance and the settlers were almost imperceptible dots. The king loved the bridges but more so the tunnels, inside which he undressed the companion with him that day while the carriage advanced through the darkness. Leaving them, he would be ecstatic from the contemplation of the highest peaks to the deepest gorges. Never before had a man come so close to the experience of a bird in flight. Because he was a sensitive man, he would often burst into tears at the sight of those amazing peaks and those inscrutable cliffs, though he didn't know whether from fear or from joy. Had he been an educated person he would have expressed his feelings in poems and songs, but he could not read; nor had he heard any music other than that of the bells clanging around the necks of goats. In a way, the Great Floating Road was his only book, which he reviewed over and over again, never tiring of studying all its details, and which, like all great books, provided him with a well-grounded education.

One night he had a distressing dream: he had climbed into his carriage to take his customary ride along the Great Floating Road, but the horses refused to move. It didn't matter that the servants whipped them until they bled: the beasts collapsed one by one rather than obey the coachman's commands. They brought a new team of horses, but they behaved in the same way. The king woke up frightened and was unable to fall back asleep.

Early the next morning the entourage set out on their customary royal excursion. This time the queen herself accompanied her husband. It was a splendid spring morning, and the king's entourage was in high spirits. The king asked the coachman if the horses had eaten well and if they were comfortable, and the man, surprised by the question, replied that they couldn't have been happier. They started on their way. The king made love to the queen in three different tunnels; the waterfalls rushed in full abundance from the cliffs; the eagles glided without moving their wings, rocked by the currents of warm air that rose from the deepest ravines; and the spring blossoms covered every inch of vegetation. Rarely had the king been so filled with joy. Suddenly, halfway across a bridge, the horses stopped dead in their tracks. That had never happened before. It was such an abrupt stop that, if the king hadn't managed to catch her in time, the queen would have been thrown out of the carriage and fallen into the void. The whole entourage rose up in panic, the king asked the coachman what was wrong, and the coachman pointed to a person blocking the way. A shepherd was walking on the bridge, behind a ram, which he beat with a stick. The first minister, who sat behind the king, asked the second minister how it was possible for that man to be there. The second minister replied that the ram had probably gotten lost and its owner had followed him over the hills. It was said that when they lost an animal, shepherds might spend a whole week in the mountains without food or water until they found it.

The carriage had started up again and was now moving slowly behind the shepherd and his ram. The first minister, furious (a shepherd and his ram stopping the royal excursion!), whispered to the king that he should have the intruder and his animal shot with arrows. There were two infallible archers in the small troop of soldiers escorting the royal retinue. But the king remembered the dream he'd had and hesitated to listen to the council of his first minister. It was a foreboding dream, apparently, and he had to be cautious. They were on one of the road's longest bridges, the ram was advancing slowly, and the royal chariot was behind, adjusting its pace to that of the animal. The ram stopped abruptly and the carriage stopped again. The shepherd whipped the ram so he would keep moving forward, but the animal wouldn't move. As if he knew there was no point in insisting, the man sat down on the road, resigned to wait for the animal's mood to change. The first minister, livid with shame, again proposed that the king command the two archers to put an end to this embarrassing incident. The king, who was a superstitious man, said that he would not interfere in the labors of a shepherd and that they needed to be patient and wait until the ram decided to move on.

He hadn't seen a shepherd since his youth. The smell of the man and the ram took him back to a time when he still enjoyed mingling with the populace. At what point had his love for the people of the plains withered and died? Or had that lofty, arrogant path been to blame for his gradual alienation from his subjects? For years, he had spoken only to his ministers and secretaries, who gave their reports on the state of the region in a timely manner, reports that he barely listened to, limiting himself to nodding his head and asking the occasional question whose answer he didn't listen to either.

An hour passed and the ram was still lying down. The shepherd gave him a distracted whipping every five minutes. The midday heat was unbearable and the servants served water to the royal family and their entourage. The king, after taking a sip, looked once again upon the pair that had blocked his excursion. The shepherd grew larger and larger in his mind until he reached the magnitude of a pagan deity. The ram seemed to him like a mythological and immortal creature. He wondered who he was and concluded that he was a simple king ruling over one of the poorest villages in China, someone who, when he died, would soon fade from people's memories. Not even that majestic work of engineering would make his name endure over time, because successive generations would regard that bold and audacious route of bridges and tunnels as something necessary and natural, a construction that, like so many others, was there because it had to be built. Everything that is, is, and there's no reason to wrack one's mind to unravel the reason for everything. That's what the king thought, and while he was thinking a strange silence made him turn his head. The queen, the ministers, and the entire entourage were asleep, including the two coachmen. They had been overcome by the heat. He also felt a slight drowsiness and closed his eyes. He opened them again when the carriage began to move. The sun had left its zenith and was already leaning toward the mountain range, casting its last rays over the peaks. The shepherd and the ram had disappeared and that deep silence remained. The king turned to look at his queen. An arrow had pierced her neck, from which a stream of blood gushed out, staining her dress and soiling her shoes. The coachman was still in his seat but leaning slightly to one side. The king touched his shoulder, and the man's body, collapsing back, revealed an arrow stuck in his chest. The king turned his head: his first and second ministers also had arrows in their necks. He stood to look at the entourage's carriage and saw a pile of bodies huddled together and motionless. Soldiers! he shouted, but received no answer. There was no trace of the soldiers. He leaned over his wife's body, looked at the arrow that had penetrated her neck, and recognized it as one of his archers' arrows. Treason! he shouted, and one of the horses whinnied, as if to answer him. Then, all at once, he understood everything. The shepherd was fake and had stopped the carriages for the soldiers to execute their slaughter, aided by the blazing midday sun that had lulled the royal entourage to sleep. The carriage was now moving forward without a driver, for the horses, at the first signs of dusk, were finding their way back on their own initiative. The king understood that he had been left alive to contemplate his own demise. The carriage was going to take him back to the castle, where the insurrectionists were waiting for him. Since there was no way to get out of the carriage, due to the narrow bridges and tunnels, if he didn't want to reach the castle, he had no choice but to jump. Thirteen bridges remained. He could choose the one he liked best.

LANDING ON THE MOON

As expected, no one stayed awake for the television broadcast in the middle of the night. They hadn't calculated that nearly six hours would elapse from the LEM's first contact with the surface of the Moon until Armstrong was ordered to exit the module and descend the ladder. Gathered in the living room of his uncle Hannibal's house, Fabricio watched how the members of his family started to fall asleep in front of the television, where the only thing that could be seen was the *Apollo 11* module resting on its four legs sunk slightly into the lunar sand.

The first to close his eyes was Uncle René, followed by his son Alfredo and the latter's girlfriend, Casandra, the only non–family member. They sat at the dining room table; all three rested their heads on their arms and fell peacefully asleep. His aunt Romina followed, a woman he was constantly running away from, because she had a penchant for giving him the most annoying kisses on his cheeks. Vero, the owner of the house, told her sister to lie down in one of the rooms, and Romina replied that if she lay down on a bed she wouldn't wake up in time to see Armstrong walk on the Moon, and that she preferred to lie down on the little Persian rug behind the armchair where Abuela was dozing off. Fabricio's other aunts, Socorro and Matilde, followed Romina's example and lay down next to her, using the sofa cushions as pillows. The rest of the family gradually dropped off, some on the couch and some on the floor, until Fabricio and his aunt Vero were the only ones still awake. The owner of the house, reluctant to follow the example of her sisters, retired to her room, but not before asking her nephew to wake her up as soon as Armstrong emerged from the lunar module, and he, who had taken the precaution of taking a little nap in the afternoon so as not to miss the moment when Armstrong stepped onto the Moon's surface, found himself, the only one awake in the family, in the midst of all those bodies lying down, like a sentinel on watch while the battalion slept.

The television broadcast had fallen into a holding pattern ever since the *Apollo 11* module had made contact with the lunar soil. The commentators had been silent for more than an hour, and amid the absolute immobility that reigned on the Moon, the only indication that this was a live television broadcast and not a photograph was the passing minutes and seconds at the bottom of the screen.

When everyone was asleep, Fabricio went to the kitchen, opened the refrigerator, and looked for the peanut butter that his aunt Vero had served as a snack a few hours before. The refrigerator was bigger than the one at his house, all the shelves overflowing with food, and he had to remove several jars and containers to find what he was looking for. He spread a generous portion of the peanut butter on two slices of bread that he then stuck together to form a sandwich, put it on a plate, and went to sit on the living room floor in front of the TV. The camera installed in one of the LEM's arms captured only a small part of the lunar landscape, but enough to perceive its infinite desolation. Among the snores in his family's improvised camp his father's and Aunt Matilde's were the loudest. He heard a whispering mumble and turned his head. It was Abuela, who was beckoning him from her armchair to come closer. Fabricio left his sandwich on the plate and, taking care not to wake anyone, stood up and walked a few steps over to the armchair where she was sitting. He knew his abuela was really sick and that the importance of such an event was the only thing that had convinced her daughters to put her in a living room chair so she could watch man's arrival on the Moon.

"You must be bored out of your mind, you're the only child here," his abuela said in her thread of a voice.

He wasn't bored, but he nodded his head so he wouldn't appear to contradict her. Abuela asked him his name and whose son he was. He told her his name and who his parents were: Osvaldo and Lorena.

"I'm forgetting names and I'm going to die," she said.

"You're not going to die, Abuela." He put a hand on her shoulder and felt the bones under her pink nightgown.

"What?"

"You're not going to die," he repeated.

She motioned for him to move his head closer and in a soft voice told him that her son Hannibal's coat was hanging on the coatrack in the entryway. His wallet was in one of the inside pockets, and she asked Fabricio to bring it to her, but to do so without making any noise. Fabricio tiptoed to the coatrack, reached into the inside pocket of his uncle Hannibal's coat, pulled out a black leather wallet, and tiptoed back to his abuela, who told him to open it and see how much money was inside. He opened the wallet, counted the bills, and told her there were one hundred and twenty pesos. Abuela told him to take out half. Fabricio took out a fifty and a ten.

"Put it in your pocket." He shook his head:
"No, you take them, Abuela."
She glared at him sternly:
"Do you want me to die right now?"
"No."
"Then you keep the money, and give it to me later."
Fabricio put the bills in the back pocket of his shorts, and his abuela motioned for him to put the wallet back where he had gotten it. He went back to the coatrack and as he was about to slip the wallet into the inside pocket of his uncle's coat, he saw that there was another pocket on the other side. He couldn't remember which one he had taken the wallet from and couldn't decide where to put it. He went back to the living room and whispered to his abuela that Uncle Hannibal's coat had two inside pockets and that he couldn't remember which one he had taken the wallet out of.

"You're smart. Put it wherever you want; Hannibal's a dumbass, and he won't notice."

He walked back to the coatrack, put the wallet in one of the two coat pockets, and returned to the living room, where his abuela motioned for him to bring his face closer and asked, her voice a whisper in his ear, if there was an orange purse on the rack. Fabricio said yes.

"It's Socorro's. Take out the wallet and remove half of what's in there," and seeing that he didn't move, she asked him: "What are you waiting for?"

"I don't like stealing."

She pointed to the plate where the sandwich was:

"You stole that peanut butter. I saw you do it."

Fabricio didn't say anything and his abuela again asked him to come closer:

"They won't notice, because I'm dying."

"You're not going to die," he said.

"Do what I told you."

He walked to the coatrack, opened his aunt Socorro's purse, and pulled out a beige pocketbook. There were several bills, including a hundred-peso note. He removed one fifty and two tens, put the wallet away, closed the purse, went back to his abuela, and showed her the bills. She nodded her approval and he put them in the back pocket of his shorts. Abuela asked him to lean in a little closer and asked if there were any other bags on the rack.

"My mom's."

"Who's your mother?"

"Lorena."

"Open her pocketbook and bring me half of what's in there."

Fabricio again refused and his grandmother turned away from him with a look of annoyance. He whispered to her that his mom knew exactly how much money she had, and she would notice if there was even just one coin missing from her coin purse.

"So you've stolen from her before." She put a hand over his and added: "Hurry up, I'm going to die."

Fabricio tiptoed back to the coatrack, opened his mother's purse, removed a black wallet from which he took a twenty and three tens, then returned to the armchair and showed his abuela what he had just pillaged. She nodded her approval and he put them in his back pocket.

"What is that?" she asked Fabricio, pointing to the TV.

"The lunar module. Armstrong will be coming out soon."

Fabricio noticed that at the bottom of the screen the hour numerals had given way to a countdown. He realized that it indicated the time remaining before the lunar module opened and Armstrong climbed down the ladder. The countdown marked three minutes and forty seconds. He leaned over to whisper in his abuela's ear:

"I'm going to wake everyone up, Armstrong's going to come out."

Abuela grabbed his arm to stop him and pointed at a cherry-colored bag hanging from the back of the chair where Casandra, Alfredo's girlfriend, was sleeping. It was a bulky purse, and it was also open.

Fabricio refused to obey her, shaking his head briskly. Unlike the bags hanging on the coatrack at the entrance, that one was in plain sight, and anyone who woke up would have caught him rummaging through it. Abuela, seeing that he couldn't bring himself to do it, turned away from him and looked at the wall.

"That's fine, I'm going to die." she muttered, and, leaning her head on the back of the chair, she closed her eyes.

Fabricio saw that there were two minutes and fifty seconds left on the countdown. He looked at Casandra's open purse and glanced around the room to make sure everyone was still asleep, and as he approached his cousin's girlfriend's chair, he felt like he was descending, like Armstrong, down a flight of steps into the unknown. His hands were sweating and he thought that Armstrong must be sweating too. He reached into the open purse hanging from the back of the chair, felt a grainy surface, and pulled out a small green wallet with a brown buckle; when he unfastened the buckle, the wallet opened, revealing two fifty-peso bills in one of the compartments. The countdown on the screen showed twenty seconds; he took out one of the two bills, put the wallet in the bottom of the purse, closed it, and walked hunched over to his abuela's armchair to show her the money. Abuela's head was still resting against the back of the armchair, and her eyes were closed. Fabricio put the bill in the back pocket of his shorts and shouted:

"Wake up, Armstrong is coming out, wake up!" Everyone opened their eyes. His aunts Romina, Matilde, and

Socorro, who were lying behind Abuela's armchair, sat up with the same expression of disbelief, as if surprised to find themselves on the floor, and their aunt Vero entered the room with a sleepy face. The rest stood up, crowding around the TV, on whose screen the LEM's hatch had just opened and the glowing silhouette of the *Apollo 11* captain was silhouetted against the black background of the lunar sky. Abuela had been forgotten halfway across the room, and Fabricio hesitated between watching Armstrong step onto the Moon and taking advantage of the fact that she was still asleep to tuck the money into her nightgown pocket. He decided on the latter, pulled the bills out of his back pocket, and stuffed them into the only pocket on his abuela's nightgown, at the moment when the family's shouting let him know that he had just missed the first human step on alien soil. He wasted precious time checking to see if there were any bills left in his pocket that could give him away, and when he turned around to approach the TV, his aunt Romina intercepted him to give him one of her suffocating kisses. Already pulling away from her hug, he tried to break through the barrier of relatives that had made a tight circle around the TV, just as Aunt Romina shouted: "Abuela's not breathing!" Everyone turned to look at her, Armstrong was momentarily forgotten, and the family barrier moved to the armchair, where Aunt Romina screamed again:

"Abuela's not breathing!" They left him alone in front of the TV and he noticed the peanut butter sandwich he had forgotten on the floor. He didn't hesitate to scoop it up and take it to the kitchen, where he gulped it down in two bites and, to erase any trace of the theft, rinsed the plate, dried it, and put it back in the cupboard. Sobbing came from the living room. He was about to leave the kitchen to finally see Armstrong tread across the fine sand of the Moon, when he realized he had left the peanut butter on the table, another revealing trace of evidence, so he opened the refrigerator to put it back in its place, trying to remember which shelf he had taken it from, whether from the second, the third, or the fourth, and decided on the third, praying to God that Aunt Vero was as stupid as Uncle Hannibal.

ARTEMIS AND THE STAG

Boris woke up late, when the sun was already streaming through the large window of the room, and it took him a few seconds to realize that he was not in his home in Melbourne. He recognized the hotel room and noticed that he was hungry. He hadn't eaten for more than fourteen hours. He'd been so tired when he arrived the night before that he hadn't even opened his suitcase. He got out of bed to go to the bathroom, and then he stopped in front of the window and looked out at the magnificent boulevard. When he opened the small double-glazed rectangle, which was the only part of the window he could open, the sound of traffic along with a blast of fresh air rushed into the room, and when he closed the glass again there was an immediate soundproofing in the room, a procedure he repeated three more times, delighting in that effect of air suction that gave him the impression of being in a submarine. It was something that he always did in all the hotels where he stayed that had double-glazed windows.

He took his toiletry bag out of the suitcase and went back to the bathroom, poured a few drops of a medicinal liquid into one of the hotel glasses, added a little water, and gargled for one minute. Then he shaved and took a shower. While he dried himself off he looked over the breakfast menu on the desk and called reception to order number four, which included two eggs any style, seasonal fruit, juice, bread, butter, jam, and coffee. He pulled the cover off the bed and spread it over the carpet; he lay down and started doing the exercises for his spinal column he did every morning. He did this for fifteen minutes. When he finished, he started to get dressed, and when he finished dressing, he checked through the messages on his cell phone.

There were two from his wife and one from his friend Walter, who was staying at his house. While he was reading them, there was a knock on the door and he went to open it. A hotel waiter said good morning and pushed the breakfast cart into the room, placed the tray on the table, and wished him bon appétit, and Boris gave him the tip he had set out beforehand. The other thanked him and wheeled the cart away. As he was eating he remembered that he hadn't checked his carry-on bag to make sure the piccolo was still there; he opened it, removed the leather case, and checked that the piccolo was there, and, after closing it, he placed it in the room's safe, returned to the table, and finished his breakfast.

The telephone rang. It was the director of the Philharmonic. They had a long, jovial conversation in English and when he hung up he felt a mild uneasiness tightening in his stomach. He arranged his clothes and shoes in the closet, put on a corduroy jacket, and left the room.

When he turned in his keys at reception, the house manager told him it was a beautiful day, one that allowed for a rare view of the sky. Boris spoke hardly any Spanish, but he understood that. He walked along the boulevard and ventured off it to explore one of the surrounding streets. It wasn't the first time he had been to Mexico City, but he couldn't say that he knew his way around. It was, indeed, a splendid morning. Had it not been for his sudden gloom, he would have enjoyed the elegance of the stores and beauty of the trees. He continued walking, and when he passed a busy café he entered, hoping the bustle would snap him out of his funk. He ordered a cappuccino that he hardly touched, and while he watched the people on the street, he decided to deal with what was bothering him. It had to do with his wife and his best friend. They were alone together in his home more than eight thousand miles away. Because he had to go to Melbourne for business, and because Susy insisted, Walter had decided to stay with them for a week right at the time Boris was leaving for Mexico. Susy had never hidden the deep affection she felt for Walter, whom she had known since middle school. He's the brother I never had, she told Boris when she first introduced them to each other. It was only the deep admiration Walter felt for him that had endeared him to this old friend of his wife's, who went from one estrangement to another, from enthusiasm to immediate frustration, with his disheveled mop of adolescent hair. Despite his failures in almost everything he did, he had somehow managed to have a fuller life than anyone Boris knew. It was as if each new setback made him more charming. And now, that perpetually immature man was in his house, staying in the guest room, and he couldn't get the image of him and Susy naked and cuddling in his bed out of his mind. He imagined her hand running through Walter's fantastic hair, which had not lost any of its abundance with age, and the image overwhelmed him. He had no doubt that Walter's hair could make any woman fall in love with him. He felt the compelling urge to walk and raised his hand to ask for the bill.

He had avoided lunch with the director of the Philharmonic, claiming to be too tired due to his late-night arrival in the city. He ate alone in the hotel, which was almost completely deserted at that hour. He was hardly aware of the wine and food and regretted turning down the Philharmonic director's invitation to have lunch together, because his company would have granted him a respite from the image of Walter and his wife frolicking in bed.

Back in his room he went into the bathroom. He tried to take a shit but he couldn't, which was what usually happened when he traveled abroad. He always needed a few days in the new country before his intestines began to trust the place. He lay down on the bed and slept for a while. When he woke up, he took another shower, since he had nothing else to do. That second shower lifted his spirits a little, and he took his time getting dressed as he watched the sun set over the boulevard. The telephone rang. Reception informed him that a man from the Philharmonic was waiting for him in the lobby. He took the piccolo case out of the safe, put on his coat, and left the room.

The chauffer for the Philharmonic barely spoke to him during the ride, which he was grateful for, as he was able to devote his full attention to the city. They arrived at the concert hall forty minutes later. A young man opened the car door for him and led him to his dressing room. Boris took the piccolo out of the case and tested the instrument's sound. Someone knocked on the door. It was the conductor of the orchestra, a corpulent man in his forties who literally pounced upon him to embrace him. He was accompanied by a short man with thick glasses, the orchestra's concertmaster, whom Boris remembered perfectly and who called him "Maestro" as they shook hands affectionately. They talked for a while in English and the conductor translated a phrase or two for the concertmaster, who nodded and never stopped smiling. Then they left the dressing room and Boris joined the stream of musicians heading to the orchestra pit to take their seats.

The hall was packed. After the brief opening piece, a rather inconsequential prelude by a local composer, the concert of *Artemis and the Stag* began. A photo of Boris appeared in the program, together with the text that described the meaning and structure of the concert. He sat next to the bassoon player, and he followed the score through the three movements, with the piccolo resting in its walnut niche. During all that time he avoided touching it so it wouldn't get wet from the sweat on his fingertips. With only a few bars remaining in the piece he could almost hear his heart pounding. The players in the brass section had finished their part and were looking at him discreetly. It was always the same in all the orchestras where he played *Artemis and the Stag*. They couldn't help but stare at him out of the corner of their eye. The score indicated that the piccolo player should stand up, without bringing the piccolo to his mouth until the last instant, so that everyone would see that he made no adjustment prior to the note being played. He moistened his lips when the violas and cellos underscored with their long and tenebrous F the anguish of the deer that comes to mate with his doe and, not finding her, sniffs the air in search of the scent of a rival buck, thus forgetting the huntress pursuing him. The cunning Artemis has been waiting for this moment to loosen her bowstring.

Boris had already risen to his feet by the time the violas had fallen silent, and from the instant he blasted that sharp, heart-rending note that pronounces the arrow shot with which Artemis kills the enamored stag, burying itself in his heart with a heavy thud, a thud similar to the suction of air through his hotel's double-glazed windows, that moment he launched it into the silence of the concert hall, he knew that the piccolo had betrayed him once again. He was a quarter note low, something the bassoonist sitting next to him probably hadn't noticed, and he was able to correct it in a split second. The entire percussion section finished off that cruel whistle with a single splendid *compás* that indicated, along with the animal's collapse, the victory of the goddess, and the audience's praise erupted throughout the hall.

As usual, he almost had to be pushed out of his chair to stand next to the conductor to receive the standing ovation. The one-note man, as he was known in modern classical parlance on the five continents, expressed his gratitude by bowing repeatedly, showing that diabolical piece of wood a few centimeters long that had awakened in the room, as it was customary to reiterate, our most ancient connection with ancient Greece.

After dinner with the conductor, the producer, their wives, and two other couples belonging to the university board of trustees that subsidized the Philharmonic, he went back to his hotel, exhausted. In his room he found an envelope from reception that had been slipped under his door. The message he had been waiting for was inside. "Tomorrow at ten o'clock." There was no signature. He wondered if she had noticed that quarter-note slip. He doubted it. Like everyone or almost everyone in the auditorium, including the orchestra musicians and the conductor himself, it was unlikely, despite their superb ear, that they would have noticed his mistake.

He woke several times during the night, and when he was fully awake, the sun already high, his head ached. At ten o'clock there was a knock on the door and he went to open it. There was no pretense, and he had to restrain himself from tearing off her blouse. They made love on the floor, just the way she liked it. Then they ordered room service, and she hid in the bathroom when the waiter came in with the cart.

They ate breakfast in bed, naked, holding hands, and when they finished he asked her if her husband had accompanied her to the concert. She replied that she had gone with a friend because Samuel had a cold.

Boris nodded.

"There's something on your mind," the woman said. "I know you. Is something wrong?"

He shrugged his shoulders in a way that he hoped would signify that it wasn't important. He freed the arm he had around her waist, flattened the pillow against the headboard as a backrest, and sat up halfway.

"Is it the note?" she asked.

"You know."

"Were you off-key?"

It wasn't the word Boris would have used. In fact, there was no precise word for that quarter-note slip; but, in essence, the concept was accurate: he was off-key.

"I'm sure that no one—"

"I know," he said, interrupting her, "but I noticed it."

"You're too demanding."

"Demanding? I played only one note the whole night, a single note, and the note doesn't come out the way it should, and I seem too demanding?"

He had inadvertently raised his voice. He noticed and asked her to forgive him.

She sat up so that she was half leaning against the headboard like him. Boris would have preferred that she stayed lying down like she was. In that position, since she was taller than him, he was a little more dominant. Not that it made him feel inferior, but the two of them being on the same level made the tone of the conversation a bit solemn, and he loathed any form of solemnity.

"You can't spend your life like this," she said.

"What do you mean, 'like this'?"

"Demanding the impossible from yourself."

"It isn't impossible," he replied with a pinch of acrimony that he instantly regretted. "I've performed that concert my whole life, I've never done anything else in my life but play that piece, I'm the one-note man, and I assure you it's not impossible, because I've done it several times. But for some time now it no longer comes out, it's as simple as that."

"Pencroff," she began...

He hated it when she called him by his last name.

"Pencroff," she repeated, as if putting her thoughts in order. "Let's suppose the note—"

"Don't suppose." He interrupted her again. "If I tell you it didn't go well, it didn't go well. This isn't an assumption but a fact."

"Okay," she said, sympathetically, "it didn't go well."

She was silent for a moment, as if she'd forgotten what she was going to say. Then she continued: "It's an awe-inspiring note."

"Ducati!" Boris exclaimed.

Giacomo Ducati, one of the most influential music critics in the United States, had been the first to call that note awe-inspiring. The adjective had become fashionable, and every time Boris heard it a chill would run up his spine.

"I know you don't like to be told that, but it's true," she said. "You can't understand it because you're on the other side, but from this one, on our side I mean, when the orchestra suddenly falls silent and you can hear the arrow shot... my God! You feel it here"—she touched her sternum with both hands—"a hollowness that shakes you, as if you were being catapulted back to Homeric times."

"Belleneuve and Taylor!" he said.

J. Belleneuve and R. F. Taylor had discussed at length, each in his own way, the archaistic spell that this note held, coinciding in defining it as the last link that that binds us to Greece.

"Forgive me, I'm unbearable this morning," he added quickly.

They remained silent; she stroked his hair and he shuddered at the touch of her hand, because it reminded him of Walter's youthful hair. Perhaps at that moment his best friend and his wife were having a chat in bed, after having made love. He asked:

"What time is it in Australia?"

"I don't know, but you should."

"I have no idea."

She turned to look at him:

"What do you mean, you have no idea? Haven't you talked to Susy since you arrived?"

"Yes, last night, before I got into bed."

"And what time was it there when you spoke?"

"I didn't ask her."

"And she didn't ask you what time it was in Mexico either?"

"No."

She couldn't hide her look of displeasure.

"Are you surprised?" he asked.

"Of course. When Samuel travels abroad and we talk to each other, the first thing I ask him is what time it is where he's calling from."

Boris was pensive. Susy never asked him what time it was in the city he was calling from and it never occurred to him to tell her either. Did that mean that they had stopped loving each other? When we love a person who is thousands of miles away and we talk to them, no matter the distances and weather, we like to imagine them in a specific place, doing a specific thing at a specific time of day.

"Do you want me to tell you what I think?" she said.

He feared she was going to tell him something about Susy that he was unaware of and his voice trembled as he said, "Tell me," a small slip that only he noticed, like the piccolo's low quarter note.

"I think you need a break. You're exhausted, sick of that note. Cancel your upcoming concerts, go back to Susy, and take a nice vacation."

He didn't like that she said "go back to Susy." He thought that was how she would tell him when she no longer wanted to be with him: "Go back to Susy."

"I can't cancel concerts; I've never done that."

"It's time you do. Stop the wheel for a while. Your note is as tired as you are. You have a real marriage with it, you know? A breather will be good for both of you. Let her frolic in the hands of others for a little while, and you do the same."

Boris looked at her, wondering again if she was aware of something he didn't know, something his wife had confided to her in one of those long intercontinental calls the two sisters had every month. Did his wife frolic with Walter? Again, he felt a tightness in his chest and felt the need to get up. He went to the bathroom, pretended to urinate, and went back to her side; she had lit a cigarette and was making smoke rings that she was blowing toward the ceiling.

"Johan would die if I canceled a concert," he said.

"Johan has composed other things," she said.

"That no one touches."

Just as he was the one-note man, Johan Máliceck, the author of *Artemis and the Stag*, had become the one-piece composer. That's why, deep down, they didn't love each other. They were attached to each other. He wondered if anyone wanted, or even loved, him, the one-note man. Strictly speaking, he couldn't even consider himself a musician. Can someone who has written only one line be called a poet? Was that Chinese man in the story a painter, the one who drew a perfect circle with a single brushstroke and never in his whole life picked up a brush again? And yet no one, in any concert hall on the five continents, had played that note like Boris Pencroff, to the extent that Johan Máliceck had decided not to authorize any performance of *Artemis and the Stag* that wasn't played by him. Ducati and the others never tired of saying that it was the most difficult note in all the repertoire of Western music: a leap into the void, without anything to hold on to. A behavioral psychologist had measured Boris's heartbeat during a performance of *Artemis and the Stag* in his native Adelaide. The heart rate curve rose gradually throughout the three movements, until, three bars before the final flurry, it steepened to reach 150 beats per minute, about the same as a hundred-meter sprinter crossing the finishing line. But what did all of that have to do with music? Many had asked that question, among them Werner Holts, who had been blunt: that note could not be played with the necessary luminosity if the performer, throughout the three movements of the composition, did not prepare it inside himself, measure after measure, until it was drawn out like some inevitable thing, a kind of birthing that couldn't be put off for another minute. The Austrian sage maintained that what at first sight seemed to be a performance that took only a few seconds in reality matured throughout the whole piece, demanding total adherence from the piccolo player to every note in the composition.

"Don't exaggerate," she said.

"Don't exaggerate what?"

"That you don't touch anything of Johan's outside of *Artemis*."

He didn't say anything because he didn't feel like talking about it. He was haunted by the image of his wife in Walter's arms. What would they be doing now?

"Do you think your sister still loves me?" he asked her point-blank.

It was the first time he'd referred to Susy as "your sister." There was an implicit agreement between them never to use that word. She turned to face him completely and he felt scrutinized to the core. A sort of lucidity, which he interpreted as disappointment, settled on the woman's features, and he watched as she crushed her cigarette in the ashtray and got out of bed.

"I'm sorry," he said, "I'm sorry."

"It's the third time you've said you're sorry. This isn't working."

"I had a terrible night," he said to justify himself.

She began to get dressed, turning her back to him. He waited for her to say something and, after a minute, trying to make his voice sound calm, he told her:

"You didn't answer what I asked you."

And seeing that she still didn't speak, he lost his cool.

"I think Walter and your sister are lovers!" he exclaimed. She continued to get dressed nonchalantly.

"Why don't you say anything?" he shouted. "Are Walter and your sister lovers? Answer me, for God's sake!"

Boris watched as she put on her blouse, sweater, skirt, and shoes, and in the midst of that silence he felt something sharp, steely, and fatal bury itself in his heart.

THE GRASS AT AIRPORTS

I'm part of the crew that takes care of the grass at our city's airport. When I say that, people are surprised, because not many people associate an airport with grass. However, all airports have grass. Think back for a moment on any time you've landed in your life. What do you see on each side of the runway, seconds before the aircraft makes contact with the ground? Grass, which you continue to see as the plane makes its wary way to its assigned gate. What happens is that no one ever pays attention to it. After a successful landing, many passengers cross themselves, others applaud, others close their eyes, grateful. Who's going to notice the grass? The same happens before take-off, when the plane builds up speed and we anxiously wait for the moment when it raises its nose and lifts off the runway.

The grass at airports is unlike the grass in parks and yards, where it occupies a servile role. It's the protagonist at airports, because there can be no bushes or trees, which attract birds, no flowers either, which attract insects, which in turn attract more birds, and we already know the great danger birds cause at an airport, as they can sneak their way into the turbines of aircraft engines. Earthworms, grubs, and all kinds of insects also thrive in the airport grass, but because it's a flat surface, with no hiding places of any kind, birds tend to avoid it; besides, they're also frightened by the roar of the planes.

You may ask, why let this grass, which needs to be mowed regularly, grow at airports when it would be easier to replace it with asphalt. It turns out that its presence is quite necessary wherever airplanes take off and land, because it contributes to the stability of air currents, untangling knots and wind vectoring that, when formed a few feet above the ground, can be one of the greatest dangers at the time of landing. It also acts as a powerful analgesic in pilots, as it is proven that when they see grass it calms them down, which is not the case if all they see is asphalt, glass, and concrete.

When I was hired at the airport, the chief of staff was surprised that someone like me, a qualified gardener who had studied in France for three years and done his internship in Europe's most important gardens, would be willing to tend the grass at an airport. I told him that I was fascinated by airplanes and that watching them take off and land overwhelmed me with excitement. Actually, I couldn't care less about airplanes. On the other hand, airport grass has fascinated me since I was a little boy. I've always been fond of those perfectly delineated stretches of turf where the grass is far from reaching the splendor of the grass on soccer fields and golf courses; grass, I would say, in a state of waiting, without a precise vocation, a bit like I was during my adolescence and most of my youth, ignorant of my aptitudes and unsure of everything. I think I loved that grass because it seemed akin to my being. So when I accompanied my parents on a plane trip and it was time to take off, instead of looking at the buildings and streets that were receding as the plane gained altitude, I would turn my head so as not to lose the last trace of the runway we had just left, and when my parents asked me what I was looking at, I would tell them that I was looking at the airport grass, which made them really sad. Look at the city, at how big it is! they scolded me, but that ocean of streets and buildings that got smaller and smaller second after second didn't speak to me. I looked at them anyway, just to make my parents happy.

I suppose my attachment to that grass is what made me want to study gardening in France and was what caused me to be that student teachers thought was so strange, since I always paid such little attention to trees, flowers, hedges, and shrubs and concentrated on the quality, distribution, and size of the grass, which my teachers and fellow students didn't care about at all. In point of fact, in parks and gardens abundant in plants and flowers, the grass is nothing more than a backdrop. Only at airports, with no masters to serve and no adversaries to overcome, does it spread out to its fullest splendor. Looking at it you can perceive the simple joy of being alive. Flowers are beautiful and, precisely because of that, they are almost dead, because they've had to resort to beauty to survive, unlike grass, which obeys a simple and unique impulse, the one that made it emerge without any difficulty in the first place, just to enjoy the sun and air.

By studying airport grass I have come to understand that gardening is not about, as many believe, extracting the most beautiful and seductive aspects from nature, but penetrating its innumerable dramas, those that manifest themselves unabashedly even in the grass alongside an air terminal. There, the grassy tapestry, uniformly maintained, clearly reveals the struggles of those who fight over the little food available. And if you think that airplanes stay out of these battles, you are wrong, because the gusts and eddies they produce at grass level are perfectly exploited by the combatants, who position themselves in the most suitable places so that their enemies are forced to climb up to the top of the blades of grass, thus being exposed to the gusts of air, which throw them and scatter them in a thousand different directions. To do so, they must know when an aircraft is about to touch down, a knowledge that earthworms, beetles, mosquitoes, wasps, scorpions, butterflies, and other airport grass dwellers have mysteriously developed. I had proof of this during the terrorist attacks a few months ago, which forced us to close the airport for three days. During that time when no planes took off or landed, we patched up various parts of the runways, the gardening team continued working as usual, and that allowed me to observe a dramatic change in the life that takes shelter in the grass. Quite simply, there was no life. Everything came to a halt: hunting, fighting, mating. In a surprising and inexplicable way, as takeoffs and landings ceased, the feverish activity that the airport's grass hides under its seemingly peaceful cloak came to a screeching halt. The birds sensed their opportunity. No longer frightened away by the roar of the engines, they pounced on the stunned and passive fauna and feasted upon them. When I saw the danger the grassy tapestry was in, I ran to speak to the head of maintenance and begged him to put up some scarecrows to put an end to such a massacre. He looked at me like I was crazy. Soon, however, the results of that slaughter became apparent. When flights resumed, the grass, without the nutriment from the components secreted by the insects, began to decay. Fertilizers, fumigations, and the introduction of new grasses were of no use. The grassy mantle was dying, exposing the earth, and dust clouds began to sweep across the airport. Whirlwinds of dust made it difficult for the planes to take off and land, until the well-known tragedy occurred. The official explanation indicates a pilot's carelessness, but the truth is different: the culprit was the huge windstorm that rose up in front of the Swiss Air jumbo jet when it was heading toward the runway with visibility reduced to a minimum.

They fired me, afraid that I was going to denounce the airport authorities, who did nothing despite having been warned about the seriousness of the problem. And that's what I did, but no one believed me when I said that the grass, the insects, and the airplanes formed a precise and unforgiving ecosystem, and the few journalists who came to interview me gazed at me in a way that reminded me of the look my parents would give me during takeoffs, when, instead of gazing spellbound at the sprawling city beneath the plane's wings, I would turn my head to look one last time at the airport grass receding beneath us.

SLOW DANCE

Every day at seven o'clock in the morning, at the bandstand in the park two blocks from where she lives, my mother takes a danzón class taught by Abraham, a young man in his thirties. Because it's a municipal initiative for senior citizens, the fee is modest (three hundred pesos per month), which I pay for, like everything else that concerns Mamá. The group began with eight women and three men, all over sixty years old, and as often happens with these kinds of activities, the initial enthusiasm began to wane, people began to stop showing up, and of the initial eleven members the only ones remaining are Mamá, Señora Evelina, and her cousin Rutilia, both of whom, in my mother's words, are "a fine bunch of people."

A couple of weeks ago my mother called me to tell me that Rutilia and Evelina hadn't shown up at the bandstand that morning and, since she was the only student, she had suggested to Abraham that he should cancel the class, but the teacher had insisted on giving the lesson, and, when they finished, my mother wanted to thank him by inviting him to breakfast at the VIPs, which is two blocks from the park. While they were having breakfast, Abraham confessed to her that he wanted to cancel the class, because the municipality paid him 80 percent of each student's fee, and since there were only three students left, it was no longer convenient for him, besides the fact that the municipality's policy was to discontinue courses that had fewer than five students enrolled. I know Mamá and I was afraid she was going to take pity on the young teacher and lend him money. I told her so, warning her that there were people who took advantage of the good intentions of the elderly. She thanked me for including her in that segment of the population (at seventy-five she still thinks she's a young lady) and assured me that Abraham was an honest young man.

I don't trust Mamá's judgment of others, because her vanity tends to blind her when it comes to assessing what a person is made of. Since her main goal in life is to mesmerize anyone who stands in front of her, all it takes is for someone to surrender to her charm to become, in turn, a charming person in her eyes.

I decided to go and see what kind of guy the teacher was, and the next day, on my way to the furniture store, I drove a few blocks off my normal route and pulled over next to the park. I walked to the bandstand, making sure my mother didn't see me, and watched the class from behind a tree. The four of them were there, Abraham and his three female students. Mamá stood out immediately; even at seventy-five she's a woman who attracts attention, and Evelina and Rutilia may be a fine bunch of people, but they don't particularly stand out because of their physical charm. Both short and chubby, wearing baggy pants and short-sleeved shirts that evidenced the stoutness of their physique, they were the perfect accompaniments for Mamá's brilliance. Bolero music streamed from two loudspeakers placed next to the bandstand railing. Mamá danced with Evelina (I knew it was her because she had told me she was a redhead), and Rutilia danced with Abraham. At some point Abraham broke away from Rutilia and took Mamá by the waist, while the two cousins began to dance with each other. I had read, I don't remember where, that a large part of the art of danzón consisted in interplay of glances between the man and the woman, in which the latter must appear elusive and subtly haughty. Mamá was not at all haughty and even less elusive, judging by the way she kept her eyes on her young teacher. He, on the other hand, barely looked back at her. I had imagined him exactly how he looked, dark and short, wearing a T-shirt and tight pants that showed off his muscles, and he moved with a smug aplomb, brushing back the loose hair that fell over his eyes in a practiced gesture. Some people crossing the park had stopped by the bandstand and I felt a little embarrassed for Mamá. She didn't dance badly, but the rapt expression plastered across her face was a bit ridiculous. The two cousins and the teacher barely smiled; in fact, they hardly looked at each other. In contrast, Mamá seemed transported to some fantasy world, and I'm sure those who stopped to watch the dance were looking mostly at her. Mamá has always made me a little sad with her over-the-top emotionality bordering on exhibitionism. When I was younger I envied my friends whose mothers were models of modesty and restraint. What I wouldn't have given to have a mom who could go unnoticed, whose face and body were ordinary and whose voice was nothing special. Mamá always seems to speak through a megaphone, and I sometimes feel like I've spent my entire life asking her to keep her voice down. You always ask me to speak more quietly, she tells me, and you don't even listen to what I say.

That night, when I went to bed, I decided that I would offer Abraham a small amount of money to continue teaching his class. I would ask him, obviously, not to say anything to Mamá. The furniture store wasn't doing well, but I told myself that the sacrifice was worth it. Since Mamá started taking the danzón class her mood had changed and she wasn't calling me off and on to complain about trivial things. I remembered her rapt expression at the park bandstand, which now, in the solitude of my bed, no longer seemed so ridiculous. In any case, I preferred that to her whiny attitude that she had worn like a second skin. I wondered if she wasn't in love with the stalky little muscular guy. At her age she still felt like a dragonfly on a summer morning.

It was half past seven when I arrived at the park; I stood behind the same tree and waited for the class to end. The cousins Evelina and Rutilia danced together, while Abraham and Mamá did the same in the center of the bandstand, attracting the attention and stares of those passing by. I could swear that no one was looking at the cousins and I wondered if those two darling women didn't loathe my mother a little. When the class was over, the four of them walked down the bandstand steps and stood there talking.

After a few minutes Mamá kissed them all goodbye and walked away down a path in the park. Watching her walk away by herself made me sad. I lived only two blocks from there, but it was the first time I observed my mother walking without her noticing my presence, and I was about to run up to meet her, to surprise her, which would have made her immensely happy. But I stayed where I was, feeling bad for suppressing an impulse that would have brought her even more joy when I told her that I'd been watching her in secret. Every time life offers me a moment of beauty, instead of embracing it, I freeze, letting the opportunity pass by, and I hate myself for my inability to act. I lost sight of her and will never forget the last glimmer of her skirt through the trees in the park. I came out of my stupid hiding place and started to follow Abraham, Evelina, and Rutilia, with the intention of approaching the little teacher as soon as he said goodbye to the cousins. I had two thousand one hundred pesos with me, which would be the monthly fees of seven students. I had to open the furniture store at nine and it was already ten past eight. We arrived at an intersection, and Rutilia gave her cousin and Abraham a goodbye kiss and headed down a narrow street; Abraham and Evelina returned the way we had come, walking faster, and they stopped talking to each other. It was clear that they were going to the same place and that they wanted to get there as soon as possible. Given the turn of events the situation had taken, I didn't know what to do, because it was clear that Abraham and Evelina were not going to go their separate ways anytime soon. I thought it would be best to retrace my steps and visit my mother, but the urge to surprise her had vanished, and with it, the desire to see her. I told myself that I should follow Abraham and Señora Evelina to find out what they were up to. I could already see Mamá's astonished face when I told her that her little teacher was sleeping with one of the cousins, if not both of them. Finally, following another sudden impulse, I decided to go after Rutilia. As I followed her I tried to imagine a reasonable motive for my decision but found none. I had to be in the furniture store in thirty minutes and I was walking in the opposite direction of my car. Rutilia, moreover, was a slow walker. I looked at my watch and told myself that if nothing happened in the next five minutes I would give up my silly pursuit and walk to my car. In my haste I had inadvertently moved closer to Rutilia, who turned her face when she heard my footsteps, looked at me, and, smiling at me, continued walking. My appearance had made her less nervous. A few steps later she stopped short, turned to look at me, and asked me if I wasn't Señora Olga's son. I blushed and answered yes, fearing that she had noticed I was following her.

"It's nice to meet you. I'm a classmate of your mother's in the danzón class. Rutilia Guzmán."

"It's a pleasure to meet you. Luis Rivadeneira," I said, and she looked at me intently while we shook hands.

"Your mother has shown us your picture several times. And you're very handsome, if you don't mind me telling you. The living image of your mother. That's how I recognized you. I said to myself: Where have I seen such a handsome gentleman? Of course, he's Olga's son!"

"Thank you very much."

"You look so much alike! She's so beautiful. People stop to look at her, you know? You should come some morning to watch us, your mamá would be so pleased."

"Yes, one of these days I'll go."

"It's a shame that the group has become so small. Now there are only three of us: your mother, my cousin Evelina, and me. The teacher is Abraham, our nephew."

"He's your nephew?"

"Yes, we call him Nene. When he was a baby we held him in our arms. He's the son of our sister Herminia, God rest her soul." She leaned forward and whispered, "He's gay."

I nodded and Rutilia looked at me with rapt attention, recognizing Mamá's features in my own.

"I live here." She pointed to the entranceway of a building. "Your mother has told us that you are a coffee drinker. I just received a sensational Veracruz espresso. Come up and try it; it will only take ten minutes."

"I'd love to, but I have to get to work."

"Ah yes, the furniture store. Tell them you're stuck in traffic; ten minutes shouldn't be a problem."

She had unlocked the gate with her key and invited me in. I was going to decline, but in the end I went in, and I think I did so because I still felt bad about not having gone to meet Mamá, and accepting Rutilia's invitation was somehow making up for that. Rutilia lived on the second floor; she had me sit in a small, brightly lit dining room and served the coffee, accompanied by some Italian soletas.

"They're my weakness. Try one."

I ate two. I told Rutilia that Mamá was afraid they were going to have to cancel the course.

"Yes, there are only three of us. Evelina and Abraham just went to talk to our cousin Everardo, to see if they can convince him and his wife to sign up. I didn't go because I don't like her. How's the coffee?"

"Delicious."

"You're the living portrait of your mother. You don't mind if I address you informally, do you?"

"Of course not."

"What a handsome son." Her eyes suddenly clouding over, she took a sip of her espresso and said, "I had a son who would be about your age now. How old are you?"

"Forty-two."

"David died when he was thirty, the same age as Abraham."

"I'm sorry, señora."

"Don't call me señora. Call me Rutilia."

"I'm sorry, Rutilia."

"It's not because he was my son, but he was just such a sweetheart." We were quiet after that. She took another sip of espresso and tried to smile.

"I'm not going to cry, don't worry. You're a sweetheart, too." She touched my cheek. Her hand was cold. "Single at your age! What a waste!"

I only smiled.

"Sign up," she said.

"I beg your pardon?"

"With Everardo, Amelia, and you, we'll have six students, and that would be enough to keep the course going."

"I can't, Rutilia, the furnit—"

"Of course you can, Luis. You'll have plenty of time to open at nine o'clock, and you'd make your mamá so happy, and us too. You're such a handsome man."

For the past month I've been going to the bandstand in the park at seven in the morning, Mondays, Wednesdays, and Fridays, to take the danzón class Abraham teaches. Now that we are three pairs, the class has taken on new vitality, and more people stop and watch us. Everardo is a nice old man who is twenty years older than his wife. Rutilia and Evelina say that Amelia married him for his money and Mamá thinks the same. Rutilia, when she dances with me, whispers "You are such a sweetheart" in my ear. Evelina doesn't open her mouth, but she squeezes my hand, which she sometimes presses to her heart shamelessly. Amelia does the same thing when it's her turn to be my partner, and she gives me, her eyes watery with desire, a pleading look that I pretend not to see. Abraham insists that I should relax my feet more and every now and then he pulls me aside and, grabbing me by the waist, takes me for a few turns in a corner, as if he wants to tell me something he doesn't want the others to hear, but he says nothing, and after giving me a little pinch on my backside, which I try to ignore, he returns me to my partner's arms. As for Mamá, she moves around the bandstand as if she were in a fairy tale.

THE ENTERTAINER

It was the offseason and there was only one cruise ship docked in the port. Fortunately, the group he was assigned to entertain was made up of senior citizens and, once the session was over, they insisted that he have a drink with them in one of the ship's bars. Contrary to his habit of not getting involved with any passengers, he accepted the invitation, perhaps because it was Friday and he had a two-day break ahead of him, or because the cruise ship was going to leave that same night and he, because he no longer worked on the high seas, would never see them again, or because he liked the fact that they didn't want to go ashore for the usual photo tour and souvenir shopping. When he asked them why they hadn't left the ship to visit the city's mosques, they laughed. To take the same pictures and buy more souvenirs that we'll throw away when we get home? they answered in chorus. A curly-haired biracial woman said that at their age it was more interesting to chat in the ship's bar sipping a whiskey and, if there was any organized entertainment on deck, join in to feel happily ridiculous singing, dancing, and playing whatever. The others nodded in agreement, raising their glasses for the umpteenth toast. He wondered how they had formed such a tight-knit group in a matter of days and, as if they had read the question in his eyes, one of the women told him that on the first evening activity of the cruise, when no one knew anyone else, she had hurt her ankle dancing the cha-cha-cha and had to go to her cabin, where she lay alone and cursing her luck. But every one of them, and she pointed to the dozen or so people surrounding her at the bar, had come to visit her, despite not knowing her, filling the cabin until there was no longer any room inside. A festive atmosphere had emerged, and so she wouldn't be left alone, most of them had refused to go to shore. After procuring a few bottles of Chianti they had spent the afternoon crammed inside those eight square meters, drinking wine and forgetting about Alexandria and its famous library entirely. The same had happened in Tel Aviv, and later in Beirut, in Nicosia, in Izmir, and even in Istanbul, the voyage's final destination. In short, none of them had set foot on land since the beginning of the cruise. If someone were to ask me for photos of this trip I'd have to show them the ones of the bottle of Johnnie Walker Black Label, the sparkling Asti, and the Beaujolais Village 2007, a lanky man said, sparking a general round of laughter.

He felt particularly at ease in the company of this group of old men and women, perhaps because of the kind of camaraderie they had formed to support each other so as to avoid getting off the ship, which gave them a vague appearance of being prisoners or carriers of some disease that excluded them from life on board the ship. At that moment, they were sitting as if they weren't completely comfortable in their chairs and were waiting for the first opportunity to take refuge in a more intimate setting. When they asked him how he had become a cruise ship entertainer, he told them that he had been doing it for a long time, since primary school, where his teacher, who was constantly called upon by the school administration, asked him to entertain his classmates during his absence. Standing in front of the group, he would tell a story he had made up on the spot, organize a game, or mime a description of professions that his classmates had to figure out. That's where he had discovered his talent as an entertainer, although he wasn't familiar with that word at the time. Years later, at a party organized by his former elementary school classmates, he learned why the teacher was absent all the time. He and the school principal had been lovers. While you were entertaining us, those two were entertaining each other in the principal's office, one of them had said. The old folks laughed, but he told them that this revelation had left a bad taste in his mouth, remembering how he was weighed down with anxiety standing in front of the group when he would run out of things to do in his repertoire and the teacher would be late in coming back. The seniors laughed again, though not with as much mirth. He explained that he was one of the lowest achievers in the class and that if he had passed the primary school level, it was mostly due to his gift for entertaining an entire class. He expected the seniors to laugh again, but they didn't find it amusing. They looked at him with a mixture of reproach and pity, and he wondered if they would judge him or think he was a fool, someone who had made his way in life by being funny. Certainly, learning that his entertaining skills had served to cover up the flings between his teacher and the principal had left more than a bitter taste in his mouth. He felt used and for that reason he had never again attended the reunions of his former elementary school classmates, who might have considered him some kind of buffoon who had earned a pass to high school because of that talent of his. Was that where he got that dourness that made him decline any invitation to events that were not part of the ship's entertainment program, such as a passenger's birthday or any other impromptu celebration? Beneath the facade of the enthusiastic entertainer, there was always the hermit who avoided joining in any kind of spontaneous celebration and as a result dampened the spirits of those who expected from him any unconditional adherence to every manner of diversion. How fortunate to have spent your life on the water, the ankle-injured woman said, breaking the silence that had momentarily descended on the group of old folks. Yes, but with my back to the sea, he clarified, and explained that a ship's entertainer must always stand with his back to the sea so that those he entertains can enjoy the view. He added that he no longer went out to sea, that after twenty-five years of working as a cruise ship entertainer he had retired in that city where he was born and there he served as a shore entertainer, going aboard ships docked in the port when the cruise ship entertainer needed a break. He entertained the passengers who hadn't wanted to disembark to visit the city, whose number was often greater than one might think, for in the latter stages of the journey many of them were tired of walking under the hot sun to visit churches, mosques, and Roman ruins. The old men and women laughed again, perhaps because they saw an allusion to them in what he said, and a chubby, calm-eyed man commented that twenty-five years of entertaining passengers was a long time. Yes, a very long time, he said, merely smiling, as if this admission embarrassed him a little, because his was a profession for young people and not for those who are getting on in years. The vast majority of those who signed up as entertainers were young people who did it for the free travel. When the cruise ship arrived at its destination, they would disembark and continue their journey overland with the money they earned on the voyage. He, on the other hand, had made the round trip from the first cruise he took: when he arrived at the port of departure, he had signed up for the next cruise, and after that, for another, always with his ear to the ground, so to speak, for some attractive job offer that never came or that, if it did, he dismissed with some excuse, because he felt at home only when he was at sea. After ten years of that life, as he was losing the energy of his younger years, he was relieved when he heard about two entertainers who had grown old on the high seas. The first, named Ricardo Gavilán, was an Andalusian who was described as a tall, wiry man, with green eyes and nervous gestures, who knew practically every dance step, was familiar with every song, seemed to speak every language, and had mastered nearly every game. A veritable meteor of enjoyment. The second, another legendary figure, was Micky, the sweetest and most delicate being that anyone might encounter on the whole planet, short and stocky, with amazing agility, who shared a cabin with his crippled mother and received no salary from the shipping company, in exchange for being able to live with her aboard the ship year-round. Ricardo and Micky had died in the same way, by throwing themselves overboard. One day Micky's mother fell out of her wheelchair, fracturing her hip and both femurs; she died in the operating room two days later, and Micky never got over it. On the first day of the cruise season he had performed with his usual brilliance, but that night, when everyone was asleep, he went on deck and jumped overboard. About Ricardo Gavilán, whose green eyes, it was said, made more than one passenger fall in love with him, it was never quite clear if he had jumped like Micky or had fallen into the sea after one of his usual solitary drinking binges in his cabin. Two different attachments, a crippled mother in one case, and alcohol in the other, had kept them on the high seas, until they became stars of their trade. As for him, after wondering about it for a while, he had given up trying to understand what had kept him on those ships, sacrificing a couple of love affairs and the possibility of starting a family for them. Even so, it's still beautiful to be on the water, said the woman with the injured ankle, and he replied that, more than the land and the sea, his favorite part was the ports, which were neither one thing nor the other but something in between, and said it was a pity that they had to leave that same night, because he would have gladly shown them the port where they were, one of the most unique in the Mediterranean. Why don't you show it to us now, while it's still light, the lanky man almost shouted. The others approved with an enthusiastic cheer and looked at him with an expectant expression, the expression he knew all too well and that more often than not he had specialized in letting down, excusing himself with any pretext to avoid any unplanned game or party that came up without warning, so that by the end of the trip they greeted him with a lukewarm handshake, when his less talented colleagues received in those circumstances hugs brimming with affection. Although the sting of these farewells hurt him, he had become accustomed to it, consoling himself with the knowledge that neither Ricardo Gavilán nor Micky, according to all those who had known them, had been popular because of their effusive character. He wondered then if it wasn't his harbor-loving soul that had prevented him from rising to the heights of his two illustrious predecessors. Perhaps he had always been a land-based entertainer, as he was now, and not a deep-sea one; perhaps he had lacked that same blue immensity in his veins that had made Ricardo and Micky great. He was about to utter the umpteenth pretext of his own, but his lips disobeyed him and something was said or nodded in a way that made the lanky fellow, who looked to all appearances like the ringleader of the group of old codgers, shout euphorically: "Well, what are we waiting for? Let's go before it gets dark!" and before he knew it they were on the gangway that was suspended over the side of the ship and climbing down to the dock, including the woman with the injured ankle, whose agility astounded him. He felt himself being dragged along by those nice old people who smiled at him, each of them in their own language, because it wasn't until that moment that he noticed they all spoke different languages, although all of them could communicate in English. And now that they were moving along together, the lanky man and the short, calm-eyed one stood out as the undisputed leaders of the group. They had rushed up to him, each one grabbing him by the arm (to hold on to him or to keep him from running away?), and the impression that he was floating made him wonder if they hadn't slipped something into his whiskey. At that hour, close to dark, there was no one in the port; the workers had left and the watchmen who patrolled the docks must have been elsewhere. Then the lighthouse came on, and its powerful light, which swept the horizon and passed over their heads, raising an exclamation of wonder in the elderly group, suddenly ushered in night, although the sky retained its evening brightness. In the midst of that kind of hallucinated somnolence that enveloped him, he wondered if it was he who was leading the group or if the group was pushing him gently along, and when it occurred to him to express that doubt to his two companions, they only smiled. It was then that he noticed the lanky man's green eyes, which he hadn't noticed before, eyes with a feline severity that women would never be indifferent to, he thought. How different from the almost heavenly gaze of the other, the short one, who was disarmingly tender! There he was, in the midst of that uneven pair, held in a manner at once gentle and energetic, and it seemed to him at times that he wasn't touching the ground because they were moving so quickly, and when the lanky man took a small bottle of whiskey out of his coat pocket and, after taking a furtive sip, put it back in his pocket, he was moved by the technical complexity of his maneuver, in which he recognized the skill of a long-suffering alcoholic, and felt like asking him for a drink, because he had not felt so at ease with strangers in a long time. But by now they had reached the shipyard, the goal of all his walks through the port, and he held back. Ahmed, the old guard, greeted him with that gesture of his with which he alluded to the inscrutable power of Allah. Access to the shipyard was forbidden, but Ahmed let him in because his family had been in debt to his for as long as anyone could remember, and besides, he always conducted his visit with the discretion of a cat. Because of that, he was afraid that Ahmed, seeing him in the company of all those people, would deny him entry to the compound for the first time. However, the old man didn't pay the slightest attention to his retinue of companions and, rising from his chair, pushed the gate open to let them pass. He imagined that the day the old man died, he would no longer have access to the shipyard, which for him was the jewel of the port, which was in turn his real city, because the other one, the one invaded by tourists from all over the world, he knew very little about, having spent his life on the high seas.

They entered the site, where they were building a large cargo ship that he had seen rising from the placement of the first beams along the keel and whose bulk drew a gasp of astonishment from his guests. The huge wooden frame, which was to serve as a mold for the assembly of the hull plates, produced the effect of the beginnings of a cathedral. Whenever he went in there, the heavy smell of paint, wood, and iron, which for him represented the essence of navigation, overwhelmed his senses. They began to walk through that enormous structure in a kind of religious silence, as if they were afraid of awakening a mythological beast. As they descended into the giant storage chambers deep inside the hull, the lanky man and the calm-looking, chubby guy kept holding him by the arms, and as they went down a very narrow staircase, he had to turn his face toward the lanky guy and felt a slight shudder at the meridional gleam in his green eyes. Behind them, the group moved in orderly single file, due to the many differences in levels that had to be negotiated. He then noticed that the chubby guy was skipping over the steps with graceful leaps, showing an agility he wouldn't have expected from someone of his build. They reached the hold that connected to the bilge, where the darkness was almost complete. Cargo ships are actual floating basements, and when you look down into the deepest holds from the deck, you feel a vertiginousness unlike that of any skyscraper. In his previous visits to the shipyard he had never reached such a deep point of a hull; he used to stop before the last holds and ascend back to the deck without ceasing to look down, bewitched by those gaps that seemed to communicate directly with the ocean floor. Now he stood between the lanky man and the plump, calm-eyed one who held him gently but firmly, both leaning over the bilge hole, whose hatch was open, and he again wasn't sure who had guided whom to that final depth. He suddenly felt a shudder at the thought that something had been poured into his whiskey so they could drag him into that hole, the most ominous part of a ship, inaccessible to the sailors themselves and where only water enters. He had let himself be fooled by the docility of these old-timers, who had come down there with very specific intentions. He thought that if he shouted Ahmed's name, the shout, amplified by the hull's resonating chamber, would hopefully reach the old gatekeeper's ears. Or perhaps Ahmed himself was in collusion with them, and that is why, when pushing the gate open for them to enter, he had avoided looking at them, something that had actually caught his attention, but he had said nothing, stunned by the speed with which they had gotten there. What ancient affront to his family could the old watchman be avenging? Were they going to throw him into the bilge, closing the hatch so he would rot in there? His two companions squeezed him a little tighter and he dug his heels into the floor, waiting for the push; but what came was a rush of nausea and the subsequent gush of vomit that spewed from his stomach and into the hole. "That's it, let it all out!" the lanky one and the stocky one exclaimed at the same time, holding him so that he could empty himself, and he heard the murmur of approval from the others behind him. He stopped retching and was led away from the bilge, and after a few steps he ran into a step, a sign that the group was starting the ascent, back to the deck. He turned himself over to his two escorts, who seemed as familiar with the bowels of the ship as, if not more than, he was, because they followed an intricate path of stairs and ramps different from the one they had used on their way down. He would ask them every now and then to stop so he could catch his breath, and even then the two would not loosen their grip on his arms. They waited for him to recover before resuming their journey, and the group followed at their heels without uttering even a whisper. When they finally reached the deck and left the shipyard, Ahmed was dozing in his chair. He glanced sideways at him, said something about Allah, and went back to ignoring the entourage that accompanied him. On the dock, on the way back to the cruise ship, he, still dizzy from being sick, obeying his entertainer's instinct that made him anxious before a silence that endured too long, asked that couple who hadn't let go of him for an instant how many cruises they had been on during their lifetime. An enormous amount, the two replied in unison. They were in a dark area along the dock and he could barely see their faces. He slowed to a complete stop and asked them if by any chance on any of their trips they had met Ricardo Gavilán, aka Richard the Lionheart, and Micky, two of the most famous cruise entertainers to have sailed the seas. He noticed an involuntary reflex in the hands of both men; at the same time he heard a murmur behind him. He turned around and saw that the others were smiling. He looked at his two custodians again and both were looking into the distance. At that moment he realized that they had already arrived at the ship. The group walked in an orderly fashion through a weighty silence up the gangway and his two faithful shadows pushed him firmly along, closing the line behind him. He tried to get out of the way, saying it was late, but his two guardian angels had a firm grip on him and he chose not to put up any resistance. It was what he had feared: the farewell celebration, with the drunkenness and the singing. Why had he agreed to have a drink with these old folks, let them seduce him with their kindness and modesty, if he knew how these gatherings usually ended? As they walked down the long corridor he asked the green-eyed man what time it was, because he had lost all track of it since they had entered the shipyard. The other didn't answer. Then he saw the sign for the restrooms and envisioned a possible way to escape. He told them that he had to pee. The two stopped and finally let go of him. We'll wait for you here, they said in unison. It was only then that he realized that they always spoke in unison. He went into the bathroom, but instead of his bladder, he emptied his stomach again, just in time to direct his vomit into the toilet. He was afraid that his guardians, hearing him, would come in to help, but the door remained closed. Now he had a perfect excuse to leave, because the vomit would excuse him from joining the party. That's when he heard the horn. He knew the ship would set sail at midnight and deduced that it was the sound of another ship's horn. He washed his face thoroughly and went out, hoping that the two old men, tired of waiting for him, had left; and indeed, to his relief, there was no one in the hallway. He didn't hesitate to retrace his steps to the door leading to the gangway, where he would finally be free. He felt another jolt of light-headedness, which he attributed to the whiskey, and had to lean against the wall to keep from falling over. Looking through a porthole in the corridor, he discovered why he had lost his balance. The ship was moving. He ran in the direction of the door leading to the gangway, and when he came to it, it was closed. He looked through another porthole and saw what he feared: the ship had sailed. Stop! he shouted, conscious of the ridiculousness of what he was shouting. He climbed a ladder that brought him to the upper deck, where he was greeted by a gust of icy wind. He walked to the railing and leaned out to look over the side of the ship, with its long, unlit row of cabins. Below, churning foam showed that the ship was leaving the harbor waters to enter the open sea. He had to go to the bridge to speak to some officer, explain his situation, tell him that he was a land-based entertainer, not an offshore one, that he had retired from cruising two years earlier, and perhaps he would agree to stop the ship so that he could get off, call for some boat from the port to come out for him, or at least allow him to get off at an intermediate port, because he knew that on a cruise ship's return voyage the ship usually sails for its home port for up to four or five days straight, without stopping. He was already seeing himself sequestered every night inside a cabin by the drunken group of elderly men and women, in the midst of their shouts, jokes, and songs. He had to go to the bridge, but he wasn't even sure he was on the main deck. There were only a few harbor lights visible in the distance. The same lighthouse as before was already a remote glimmer. He looked at the wide wake formed by the ship, which now advanced at full speed into the blackness of the night, a black so dense that he could only guess, without distinguishing it, the vastness of the sea, and, before jumping, he sensed, like a good entertainer, its infinite embrace.

EXTRAS

It's no easy task to find Vladimir Pencroff in all the films he has acted in. We see him fleetingly in *A Diamond for Eleonor* (2001), in the office of a small newspaper, talking on the phone on the left side of the shot, while in the foreground Kathy Bates and Paul Giamatti discuss the article the former has just written. In *Submerged* (2007), which re-creates the disaster of the Russian submarine *Kursk*, he is one of the five crew members who plug a water leak in the ship's command room. He earned the honor of a close-up in *Back from the Clouds* (2004), as one of a crowd of people looking up to admire the aerial acrobatics of five fighter planes during the Independence Day celebrations in the United States. The latter was, without a doubt, his most prominent role. In his other film appearances he is a nearly invisible figure: he crosses the hallway in an office, claps his hands in a crowded concert hall, disappears into an elevator, sips an alcoholic drink at a bar counter, or is just another customer in line at a bank window.

Vladimir Pencroff belonged to the California Association of Film Extras and Figurants, which provides about

30 percent of extras for American films. He appeared in more than ninety films shot in and around the Los Angeles area, and was unable to appear on set on only one occasion, because he had bronchitis. During the fifteen years he worked as an extra, he never shook hands with a leading actor or actress, let alone a director. Now, thanks to *Extras*, the film that marks his successful debut as a director, we know that when the extras arrive on the set of a film they must occupy a certain place, and a coordinator tells them where and how they have to move. Once the scenes have been filmed, another coordinator gives them an envelope with their payment and, if necessary, schedules an appointment for them to come back for another day of filming. One of these coordinators became famous because when handing the envelopes to the extras, he used to shake their hands enthusiastically and exclaim "Good job! Good job!" when all they had done was cross a street or sit in a hospital waiting room. The phrase became famous after that and since then the coordinators for the extras are called "Goodjob."

Extras pretends to be a documentary about the filming of a movie entitled *A Strange Couple*, which narrates the collapse of a marriage when the husband catches his wife kissing a stranger on the street. The story told in *A Strange Couple* is reduced to the arguments between husband and wife following the discovery of her infidelity. We see them fighting in their living room, in a restaurant, on the street, in the middle of a field, inside an elevator, or in a gym. We get only a few snippets of these quarrels, because the camera gets distracted and immediately leaves the couple to move to another place, looking at people, buildings, trees, and even the sky; in short, snooping here and there, while the voices of the man and the woman fade away until we stop hearing them altogether; then, as if remembering its duty, the camera returns to the couple, who continue arguing, but only to start again a minute later its wandering around the surroundings, as if bored with what it has just seen and heard. These camera excursions represent the crux of Pencroff's film and exemplify his notion of cinema, which he expressed in an interview in these words: "If a dead man had the chance to come back among us to enjoy a few moments of life again and the only thing he would be granted was to watch a movie, he would hardly notice the actors in the foreground, because their words, their gestures, and their looks wouldn't tell him anything he didn't already know. Instead, he'd be attracted to the extras who, almost out of frame, move their mouths without us hearing what they say, laugh without us knowing the reason for their laughter, greet others, pay a bill, open a window, or close a door. Imagine, in that profusion of unimportant gestures, how much life is encompassed there for him who no longer enjoys life!"

Pencroff wants to show us the depth of our simplest acts, which is why in his film he pays particular attention to the performances of the extras. In the office where the unfaithful wife's husband works, these performances are resolved in a ballet of precise movements: the extras try not to get in the way of the main actors and try not to get in each other's way either. Their gestures are banal (walking, talking on the phone, taking a sip of coffee, greeting a colleague), but their repetition shows us how inconceivable our life is without them. It's surprising to see, for example, how something as simple as making a photocopy manages to affect us when we see this action repeated five or six times. There's the woman who places a sheet on the glass, lowers the lid, presses the start button, waits a few seconds while the scanner light sweeps over the sheet, and removes the photocopy that comes out of the bottom tray. She is only one of the extras who move around the office, and once the actors enter the scene, we will hardly notice her, but now, her actions next to the photocopier, repeated over and over again in the performance prior to the shot, acquire a more profound meaning than we expected. We think: how beautiful life is, how the dead must envy us, and what wouldn't any of them give to make a photocopy in an office, like that woman! In fact, we make a point to do the same as her as soon as the opportunity presents itself, certain that the simple act of making a photocopy, if we pay the proper attention to it, will bring us a wealth of happiness. Actually, the performances that Pencroff places in front of our eyes, made up of insignificant gestures and actions, convince us that if we always conducted ourselves like extras in a movie, taking the greatest care in everything we do, even the most insignificant things, our life would be immensely happy.

We can deduce from all this that for Pencroff, cinema is essentially a happy art, because the life that bustles around the characters never ceases to seep into the scenes.

It is an art that is, by its very nature, overflowing, if not with people, then with objects, which always appear in excess for the specific purposes of a shot, so that any conflict or adversity experienced by the characters will be attenuated by being set against a background of things and people unrelated to their passions. The extras, therefore, are more than just simple decor; they are, on the contrary, an active part of the story, the proof that life goes on and that its mighty torrent will eventually absorb or minimize personal heartaches and misfortunes. Without that torrent, life would be meaningless, and Pencroff shows us this in what is perhaps the most emblematic scene of *Extras*, where the husband and wife are arguing in the middle of a crowded bus station. Suddenly, the surrounding crowd of extras stands still, as if frozen, while they continue their bickering. The sudden immobility of all the extras makes the couple's gestures, torn away from the movement and bustle of the station, seem ridiculous and without substance. We understand that extras are the binding agent without which no one life can truly connect with another. The scene is long, because the camera lingers for a few seconds on each of those extras, stopped as if by some kind of magic. When he could have resorted to a computer-generated trick freeze, Pencroff preferred a human, *acted* immobility. So what we see is all those extras playing the role of statues: they breathe, blink, move slightly, and it's inevitable to think that for the first time they are really acting, earning that close-up bestowed only upon actors. Pencroff, no doubt, wanted to pay tribute in this way to his former colleagues in the Californian Association of Film Extras and Figurants, almost all of whom were invited to perform in this crowded scene, but the unusual close-up of their faces is more than a tribute to an unfairly underappreciated craft. Those faces are ours, those extras represent all of us, who are the extras of countless stories that take place next to us without us being aware of them. Our life, Pencroff seems to tell us, consists most of the time of being extras crossing a hallway, crossing a street, turning a corner, opening a door, or going down in an elevator, happy to be alive and unaware that we are. Something like this affirms the only extra who talks about her trade in the film, a mother who says: "When I go to the movies to see myself, I break out in a sweat. That woman in the background, carrying a flowerpot, is that me, I wonder, because I don't recognize myself. I see a happy person, totally alive."

After the success of *Extras*, Pencroff ceased to belong to the California Association of Extras. Multi-award-winning and widely photographed, his face no longer meets the essential requirement of an extra, which is to be anonymous. It's as if someone wanted to hire Robert de Niro or Meryl Streep as an extra, said the association's secretary, when asked why Pencroff had been suspended from the organization. Half-jokingly, Pencroff stated in an interview that if he had known that he would no longer be able to act as an extra because of his film, he wouldn't have made it. "I never imagined that the movie would be as successful as it was. I'm glad, but I'm also disappointed, because I won't ever be able to step on a movie set again, doing the only thing I know how to do well, which is to move around without looking at the camera." As it is, Pencroff will be able to return to a film set only as a director, but when asked if he was working on a new project, he replied that he wasn't cut out to direct films and that *Extras* represents his film debut and his farewell to it. However, everything seems to conspire to contradict that. *Zoom* magazine, following the success of *Extras*, interviewed several Hollywood stars to ask them if they would be willing to act for free in a movie in which they would appear only as extras, and the responses have been incredibly enthusiastic. Robert de Niro said: "I'd love to. I think I'd be an excellent extra." Julia Roberts stated: "I wouldn't hesitate for a second. Just the thought that I wouldn't have to learn any lines and it would all come down to taking a few steps on a street or in a hospital corridor makes me really happy." Brad Pitt, likewise, confessed: "I'd be thrilled to do it, because in every actor there's a hidden extra that peeks out at even the slightest opportunity. I've played the role of an extra many times without the director or the other actors realizing it." Meryl Streep: "I've lived among extras my entire professional life. They're the ones who give me the strength to do what I do. When I'm struggling with a scene where it's just me and another actor, I imagine that we're not alone, but surrounded by extras, and with that simple trick I almost always find the right tone." *Zoom* also asked them who they thought would be the most suitable director to shoot a film where the extras would be famous faces and the actors complete strangers, and they all gave Pencroff's name without any hesitation. When he heard this, Pencroff stated:

"Maybe I'll actually take a stab at filming it, including myself in the cast. It would be the only way I could go back to work as an extra."

MURDER IN THE GLADIOLUS

One of Ernesto's colleagues had recommended that little hotel located on the less frequented part of the Bay of Huatulco. From the moment they arrived, he and Irene had been raving about the tasteful decor and the beautiful beach view from the room's balcony. Irene had grouped her vacation days into a single week, and Ernesto, who was still leading screenwriting workshops, only had to schedule his classes together the week prior to their trip so that their little foray to the beach wouldn't mean a reduction in his income.

They'd been living together for three months and it was the first time they could afford to take a vacation. Irene had brought a detective novel by Edward Mulligan; she'd already read fifty pages and she was hooked from the start. They'd dreamed of being alone together by the sea, swimming, reading, eating, and of course, making love. However, at breakfast the day after their arrival, Ernesto ran into Gordo—his name was really Arciniega, but they always called him Gordo because he was so chubby—his old screenwriting teacher from film school, and because he was by himself, the couple felt obliged to ask him to join them at their table. Gordo told them that he was quite familiar with the hotel; he used to spend his vacations there that time of year, and after his wife's death the year before, he had wanted to return to the place she loved so much. Ernesto offered a few words of condolence, for which Arciniega expressed his gratitude. Irene said that she had fallen in love with the hotel the moment they walked into the lobby and she planted a big kiss on Ernesto's mouth. This trip is like our honeymoon, she added, as if warning Arciniega that they had come to be alone. Gordo congratulated them and, seeing the Mulligan book on the table, he said that a version of that novel had been made into a film five years earlier, though it wasn't very successful, because the plot revealed that the chauffeur was the murderer too soon, while in the novel that fact was kept hidden until the final pages. Irene looked at him dumbfounded and waited for him to say he was joking. But Gordo Arciniega, far from doing that, commented that this mistake had cost the screenwriter two juicy contracts with Universal Studios: they'd been canceled. She looked at Ernesto, and, seeing that he was avoiding her eyes, she squeezed his leg so that he would turn to look at her. She was furious with that stupid man Arciniega, who had shredded the mystery of the book, and she needed Ernesto to say something, or to look at her at least. But Ernesto didn't pay her the slightest attention and continued to listen to his old teacher's comments. Irene withdrew her hand and while she looked at the garden through the large window, she remembered that Ernesto had sent his latest script to a contest for which Arciniega served on the jury. She realized that he was careful not to let Arciniega know how inappropriate his comment was so he wouldn't get on his bad side, and she looked at Ernesto as if seeing him for the first time, and an icy fury seethed through her at the evidence of having fallen in love with such an opportunist. She stood up from the table, murmuring a faint "Excuse me," and returned to the room.

When Ernesto finally caught up with her there, he was holding Mulligan's novel in his hand and told her that she had forgotten it in the dining room. Irene, who had been lying on the bed staring at the ceiling, got up, ripped the book out of his hands, and threw it over the balcony railing. He flinched at the violence of her gesture and told her that it wasn't his fault that Arciniega had been so stupid as to reveal the identity of the murderer. Irene, who had gone back to the bed, jumped up to shout at him that he was both disloyal and cowardly, and so that he wouldn't have any confrontation with his old teacher and compromise his chances in the screenplay contest, he had ignored her, not caring that the arrogant idiot had spoiled the mystery of her novel. Her voice cracked and she began to cry with such rage that Ernesto, who had wanted to hold her in his arms, didn't dare touch her and noticed a hatred in her sobs that terrified him. He went out to the balcony, hoping she would calm down, but the view of the sea ended up spoiling his mood. It flashed so intensely in the midday light that it looked as if it could have come right up to the hotel at any moment and swallowed him up. As he leaned on the balcony railing, his gaze wandered around the garden surrounding the block of rooms and he spotted Mulligan's novel among some gladiolus bushes. He realized that they still hadn't gone to the beach, and he thought that the silly quarrel caused by his teacher's clumsiness would be forgotten as soon as they sank their feet in the surf washing up along the shore. Irene, in the meantime, had gone into the bathroom, and when she came out she was wearing a pink two-piece bathing suit that accentuated the beautiful curve of her waist. Her face had hardened into a weary grimace; she stood in front of the mirror, arranged her hair, and said that she was going to the pool to lie in the sun. We should go to the beach, he said. She said that it was too windy and she didn't want to get sand in her eyes. Then I'll go by myself, Ernesto replied, thinking that he would convince her to join him that way, but Irene wasn't fazed and with a terse "Do what you want," she left the room. He, instead of going down to the beach, took a chair out to the balcony and sat looking at the sea, knowing that if he went to the beach for the first time without her, things were going to get worse.

Later they ate at a seafood place about a block from the hotel. They hardly spoke as they were eating, and once they were back at the hotel they were grateful for the heavy downpour that spared them from having to make decisions about what to do and where to go. Ernesto didn't go up to the room and he told Irene that he was going to the dining room for coffee; instead he went out to the garden to look for the Mulligan novel. He rescued it from the middle of the gladiolus, completely soaked; then, drenched from head to toe himself, he went into the dining room and sat at a table next to the bay window. He was the only customer. He had hoped to find Gordo Arciniega, so he could talk to him about movies and drop the hint that he was competing for the screenplay prize Arciniega was not only judging but also presiding over. He ordered a cappuccino, picked up a *National Geographic* from the magazine rack in the entryway, and read the entire magazine, holding the Mulligan novel open on the table so it would dry out. When he went up to the room, the book was still damp and he decided to leave it in his backpack, so Irene wouldn't see it. She was lying down watching a cooking program on the television, and he went to take a shower. When he came out of the bathroom he threw himself onto the bed and while he watched the same program sleep got the best of him. By the time he woke up it was already dark, the rain had subsided; they got dressed and went out for dinner. Ernesto said that Arciniega had recommended a restaurant three blocks from the hotel where they made a delicious grilled octopus, but she said that he'd probably be there and that she didn't have the slightest desire to see him. They ended up having dinner at a taqueria with charcoal-grilled meats, and he thought that coming to that beach to have dinner at a taqueria like thousands of others in Mexico City sealed up that depressing and pointless day with a sad ending. Back at the hotel they watched some

TV again and went to bed early, at an hour that would have otherwise seemed unheard-of if they hadn't been upset with each other.

The next day he went down to the dining room a little before she did. He was the kind of person who, after opening his eyes, couldn't go five minutes without coffee; he put a magazine and his reading glasses in his backpack, and he told her he'd wait for her to have breakfast. When he walked into the dining room he saw Gordo Arciniega, who invited him to sit at his table. They talked for a while, and when she appeared, Arciniega himself raised his hand to call her over. Irene greeted him with a curt "Good morning," and went to the buffet line for a bowl of fruit. When she got back to the table, she was alone with the screenwriting professor because Ernesto had gone to get his breakfast, and Arciniega asked her how her night had been. She replied that it had been good and refrained from asking him the same question. Arciniega touched his forehead, as if remembering something, and told her that the movie he had mentioned to them the day before wasn't based on the Mulligan novel she was reading but on another one by the same author, the title of which he couldn't remember. I'm getting old. I never made these mistakes before, he said while he chewed on a piece of bacon. Irene replied dryly that he had said the killer was a chauffeur and it just so happened that there was one in the novel that she was reading. Arciniega smiled and said that there was a chauffeur in every one of Mulligan's novels. I forgot something in the room, she said, then got up from the table and left the dining room, walked through the pool area, and, coming to the block where their room was, looked for the novel among the gladiolus and roses. One of the groundskeepers was watering the lawn and saw her rummaging through the bushes, but he didn't go over to ask her what she had lost. Discouraged, she went to the reception desk and asked the manager if someone had found a book in the garden under the balcony of her room. The man picked up the phone, dialed a number, spoke with someone briefly, hung up, and told her that no book had been found. Irene went back to the dining room. She was relieved to see that Ernesto was alone, had finished eating, and was waiting for her. She sat down beside him and started eating her interrupted breakfast, and he, without her asking, told her that Arciniega had gone up to his room to pack, because he was flying back at noon; then he asked her where she had gone and she told him that she had gone to the garden area to look for her book, and since it wasn't there, she had asked about it at the front desk, but no one knew anything about a lost book. She told Ernesto what Arciniega had said and he remarked that he wasn't surprised, because in his classes he was always making mistakes by changing the titles of the films and mixing up the names of the actors in the cast. She got up to go back to the buffet for more breakfast, and when she returned to the table, Mulligan's novel was to one side of her glass of juice. She opened her mouth in surprise and Ernesto, smiling, told her that he had rescued it the afternoon before, on his way back from lunch. Grateful, she gave him a kiss on the cheek and told him that it must have gotten soaked in the downpour. He said it had and asked her if she forgave him. Irene pursed her mouth and nodded her head. It wasn't the most charming gesture in the world but they had made their peace. I'm glad that he left, she said afterward, and Ernesto was quiet. Irene asked him what was bothering him. Nothing, he said, but she didn't believe him. There's something you're not telling me, she said. He sighed in reply: Arciniega read my script and he didn't like it. Arciniega's an asshole, I told you, Irene exclaimed. Ernesto remained silent, then said that the script had a serious flaw and Arciniega, who was no idiot, had brought it to his attention. It had to do with the dialogue. Arciniega had liked the story, but the dialogue, according to him, was the weakest he had ever read. Gordo had offered to rewrite the script with him, because he thought the plot had a lot of potential. If it were ever to be filmed, they would share the credits. Did you accept? Irene asked. Ernesto said that he had never been good at dialogue and Arciniega's skill in that area was legendary. Legendary? she repeated sarcastically, and exclaimed: You admire him too much and he's taking advantage of you; tell him to go to hell, work harder on your dialogue, and don't share your story with anyone. They stood there in silence, looking out at the shoreline. Out of the blue she said that she didn't like the hotel; the employees weren't very friendly, the breakfast was little more than average, and the decor was tacky. You said you liked it, Ernesto replied, and then they were silent again.

They spent the whole day on the beach. Irene sunbathed, then she cooled her feet in the water, sunbathed again, but not once did she open the novel. In a little restaurant along the beach they ate a blacktail bream that she found bland. The beach itself, which looked spectacular from the hotel, no longer seemed like such a big deal to her, and now she understood why it was almost deserted. That's its charm, Ernesto said, why would I want a spectacular beach crowded with people. That afternoon, in the same restaurant, they got a little drunk on mojitos and beer. Ernesto tried to kiss her, but she didn't let him. The cook keeps looking at us, she said. Let her look, he replied. Irene finished her mojito and shook her head in a way he knew didn't augur anything good. He asked her what was bothering her and because she didn't say anything, he gulped down his beer, turned to the cook, and asked her for another one in a commanding tone that Irene didn't like. You're drunk, she told him. Because I want to kiss you I'm drunk? he replied, raising his voice. She turned and looked toward the horizon; the sun had just set and the sea at that moment seemed like a strange, imposing presence, detached from everything. She didn't like that hour of the sea when the darkness, incomplete as it was, gave off some kind of bad omen, and she wanted to go back to the hotel. You go ahead, I just ordered another beer, Ernesto told her. She got up and left.

Everything they said in the room in the hours after that was tainted by a misunderstanding; what for Ernesto was a new and tempestuous discussion, for Irene was simply a farewell. It took him a while to realize that, and when he did, he fell into an almost hypnotic trance. It was as if Irene had been transformed into a specimen from another planet. He had the feeling that he was seeing her entire being for the first time, something he had not managed to do in the three months they had been living together. While she moved around the room packing her things, which she had unpacked hardly two days before, he watched her with the fascination of one who is watching a staging or a dream, and so, after crying, he began to laugh, as if he too were acting on a stage.

Irene and Arciniega met a year later in the home of a mutual friend who was throwing a party to celebrate the premiere of his new play. It was Arciniega who spotted her among the crowd of guests and went over to greet her. Here's our Mulligan fan, he said, clinking his wineglass with hers. Irene was with an attractive young man, whom she introduced to Arciniega as a painter, and, after introducing him, she kissed him on the mouth. They exchanged a few words, then someone approached to greet the young painter, who then moved away from them a little, and Arciniega took advantage of that opportunity to ask Irene if she knew anything about Ernesto, saying he hadn't seen him since they had met a year before at the hotel in Huatulco. Irene replied that she hadn't seen him since then either and that she hadn't heard from him at all. There was a brief silence and Arciniega told her that he owed her an apology for spoiling Mulligan's novel by telling her who the murderer was. Irene told him that it didn't matter, as he himself had later clarified that he had been thinking of another one and that the film was inspired by another one of Mulligan's books. So you didn't finish reading it, Arciniega said. She admitted that she hadn't finished it and asked him how he knew. Because I lied to you, Arciniega exclaimed, and told her that the movie was indeed based on the novel she was reading; however, Ernesto had asked him to tell her that he had been mistaken, and when he pointed out that she would be upset when she discovered that the killer was really the chauffeur, Ernesto had told him not to worry, because his girlfriend would most likely not even make it halfway through the book. The color drained from Irene's face. Arciniega realized this and regretted having spoken to her about it. From what I can see, I've screwed up a second time, he exclaimed. She took a sip of wine and asked him why Ernesto was so sure she wouldn't finish reading the novel. Arciniega told her that he had asked Ernesto the same question. And? was all Irene managed to articulate, a lump growing in her throat. He took another drink before answering and told her that Ernesto's answer was simply that she was like that. Like what? Irene asked, clenching her glass. Someone who, after a brief period of excitement and exhilaration, became disillusioned with everything: books, places, and people, Gordo Arciniega replied.

TIME TO TAKE OUT THE TRASH

The lady from the real estate agency who showed him the apartment, after extolling the balcony overlooking a park, the high ceilings, and the light-filled rooms, opened a metal hatch located on one of the inner courtyard walls, next to the kitchen, and told him it was the garbage chute. You can drop your garbage bags here and voilà! she exclaimed. While she talked, Ricardo turned his attention to a Bach piece that was coming from the adjoining apartment and asked who lived there. The woman didn't know. It was the music, more than the balcony or the high ceilings or the garbage chute, that made him want to rent the apartment, because having cultured neighbors promised peace and harmony.

He ran into the woman one afternoon when he opened the metal hatch to throw out the previous day's garbage. She had just opened the hatch on her side, and in that way, through the garbage chute, they met. They were both a little shocked seeing each other like that, and she was the first to snap out of her surprise. She asked him if he was the new tenant who had just moved in and Ricardo said yes, he was. Welcome, she said, and he thanked her. The hatches were large enough so they could see each other's face and part of their bodies. The woman was in a wheelchair, holding a garbage bag, and she was wearing a nightgown that closed around her neck. Ricardo guessed that she must have been about seventy-five years old. With her there, on the other side of the garbage chute, he hesitated to throw his garbage bag in, and the woman sensed his reluctance, because she told him he should just drop it in. He dropped the bag, which plummeted to the basement floor four stories below. Then the woman stuffed her bag into the chute and let it fall. There's a strange smell today, she said. She sniffed the duct, making a noise with her nose, and backed her wheelchair up a little, leaving the hatch open, apparently ready to continue conversing through that meter-wide gap that connected the two apartments. They fumigate every fifteen days; it shouldn't smell like that, she said. Ricardo noticed her foreign accent and asked her where she was from. From Ireland, she replied. He told her that he was learning English online, because he was supposed to go to Australia in three months and he would be there for six weeks. His company's headquarters was in Melbourne. The woman, who hadn't understood him very well, wheeled closer to the garbage chute and asked him to speak louder. Ricardo repeated what he had just said. She sniffed the chute again. It smells so sharp today, she said, adding: Don't mind me, I have a sensitive nose; I'm going to call the fumigator and ask him to spray again, and she asked him how good his English was. He replied that it was spotty, especially his grammar. Forget about the grammar, what you need is conversation, she said, and Ricardo agreed. The woman had backed away again to get away from the stench. I'm going to call the man who sprays, she repeated, and after wishing him a good day, she closed the hatch to her side of the garbage chute. Ricardo closed his and stood there but didn't move. He'd lacked the courage to suggest that she could give him conversation classes. She was clearly an educated woman and English was her mother tongue. Besides, she lived on the other side of the wall and all he would have to do was cross the landing to attend his classes. He heard her open her duct hatch, most likely to toss in another garbage bag, but instead he heard the sound of her nose sniffing the chute. She's obsessed, he thought. He opened his duct hatch and the woman pushed back with a start. Ricardo apologized for scaring her and, without preamble, asked her if she would be willing to give him some conversation lessons. She looked him in the eye, inhaled, and pushed back again. She seemed to be considering his proposal. Ricardo added that he would pay her, because the classes would be paid for by his company. He looked at her hands, furrowed with thick veins and laden with rings, and he thought that she must live alone. The woman came out of her musings and told him that she would have loved to, but her husband was a difficult person, he was sick and didn't like to have anyone in the apartment; he didn't like her going out either. I understand, he said, and he asked her to let him know if she changed her mind. My name's Ricardo, he added. I'm Caroline, she said. Nice to meet you, Ricardo said, and gently closed the duct hatch.

At another point in his life he wouldn't have agreed to go to Melbourne, but after breaking up with Marisa, spending time on the other side of the world was exactly what he needed. They'd been dating for two months when she called him one night to tell him that it would be better for both of them that they stop seeing each other. They had incompatible temperaments, she told him. At first he thought she was joking. He had rarely felt so in tune with a woman as he did with Marisa, and the explanation that they had incompatible temperaments sounded like something out of a soap opera. He asked her if they could meet. She told him she couldn't, that she needed time to figure out her feelings for herself. Ricardo asked her if there was someone else, and Marisa was so vehement in denying it that he believed her; but knowing that there was no other man in her life, far from being a relief, made him even more confused, because it could only mean that he had turned out to signify hardly anything to her at all. He waited two weeks before he called her back, hoping that things had shifted in his favor, and when he did, she stood by her decision, now treating him with a distance that cut him even more deeply. It was her tone of voice that he didn't recognize and he knew then that it was all over and that he would never know the real reason for her inexplicable behavior. So when Suárez, the company's director, asked him if he would be interested in spending six weeks at the company's headquarters in Melbourne to familiarize himself with the new machinery that was to replace what they currently used, he agreed without hesitating.

Back from work, when he opened the hatch to throw out his garbage, he found Caroline's face on the other side of the garbage chute. They greeted each other and Ricardo had the impression that she had been waiting for him. She was farther back from the duct than the day before and was wearing a floral nightgown that was slightly open, exposing her neck. I've noticed that you always throw your garbage out at the same time, she said. Ricardo admitted that he was a creature of habit and dropped his garbage bag, which landed with a heavy thud four stories below. The other told him that she had been waiting for him, because she wanted to know if his offer from the day before was still open. Since her husband, Osvaldo, she explained, had become ill, because of his medicine and treatments, things were a little tight and a little extra money would help them out. So your husband is okay with this, Ricardo said. No, of course not, she said, and she clarified that she hadn't asked him, because she was sure he wouldn't approve, but she had found a way to keep him from finding out, which was to have the classes right there, opening the two chute hatches. Her husband hardly ever went into the kitchen, let alone near the inner courtyard; in fact, he hardly left his room, except to go to the bathroom and walk up and down the hallway for a while. Ricardo didn't say anything. He had no interest in having an English class across a garbage chute. The woman, as if she had read his thoughts, told him that if they moved away from the chute, they wouldn't smell the stench. Let me think about it, he said. She smiled; Ricardo gently closed his chute hatch, returned to the kitchen, and thought: She's crazy.

The next day Suárez sent for him. His boss was in a bad mood, said he had a bad cold and asked him to keep his distance. He informed him that there had been changes regarding his departure for Melbourne. He would have to go alone, since Villegas wouldn't be able to go due to certain family matters. That wasn't all: the trip had been moved up and he had to be in Melbourne in a month and a half. The first part was good news, because he didn't like Villegas and he didn't like the idea of being stuck with him during the trip; also, the fact that they were sending him by himself, without his immediate boss, represented a symbolic promotion, because the company was placing all the responsibility of becoming acquainted with the new machinery on him. The second, however, was bad news: he had only a month and a half to improve his English. He told Suárez, who shrugged. They were orders from the head office, he told him, and if he didn't get his act together, they would send Cáceres, who would be more than ready to do it. Ricardo didn't hesitate and said he would go. Back home, he opened the chute hatch to toss out his garbage and then hit the door on the opposite side three times with a broomstick. It didn't take long for it to open and Caroline, who was wearing the same nightgown as the day before, greeted him with a broad smile. Ricardo told her that his trip to Australia had been moved up. In light of that fact, they could try the classes like she had mentioned. She suggested an hour a day, at the same time, when he came back from work. When it was time to take out the trash, she said, smiling. Yes, at trash time, he agreed, serious.

He bought a notebook to write down the most commonly used colloquial words and phrases that came up in the classes. He was pleasantly surprised by Caroline's knowledge. She was an intelligent woman, with a sense of humor, knew how to carry on a pleasant conversation, and she corrected his pronunciation with gentle assurance. She asked him things about his life without excessive curiosity and one afternoon he couldn't help it and in his poor English he told her about Marisa. He wanted to know what she thought about the matter. Caroline asked him if the same thing had happened with other women and Ricardo replied that it had one other time, although not in such an abrupt way. Caroline was mulling over an answer and finally told him that on his trip to Australia, away from Marisa, things he was now unable to understand would become clearer to him.

He paid her once a week, putting the cash in an envelope that he slipped under her door, after alerting her with two taps on her chute hatch, so that she would pick up the money before her husband found it on one of his excursions down the hallway. Using the same method, only with three taps instead of two, he would ask her for some idiomatic or pronunciation clarification, which Caroline would solve immediately, without opening her door completely and speaking to him hurriedly, fearing that her husband would show up. On one occasion she lent him a children's book in English, and because it was too thick to slide under the door of his apartment, she put it in a plastic bag she tied closed with a string, the opposite end of which she tied to her wrist, and threw it across the garbage chute approximately three times, until he finally managed to catch it.

They never spoke of Marisa again, and as the date of the trip approached Ricardo had the feeling that Caroline wanted to tell him something but couldn't find the courage or the right moment to do so. He asked her if she was happy with the amount he was paying her, to which she replied: "Oh, absolutely!" In fact, he paid her almost double what other language teachers were paid. More than once he caught her sniffing her arms and the fabric of her nightgown with a covert gesture and thought she wanted to make sure that the stench coming from the garbage chute hadn't lingered on her.

The day before his trip, Suárez told him he didn't have to go into the office so he could take his time packing and preparing for it. Midmorning, his doorbell rang. It was the fumigator, a man he had never seen before. Ricardo opened the chute hatch, and the man sprayed the inside of it with disinfectant. The guy told him that he had never had the pleasure of meeting him, and Ricardo explained that he was never at home in the mornings. The other told him not to worry, because from his neighbor's apartment, Señora Caroline, he was able to use his device to spray down his chute hatch, although not as effectively as he was doing now. Señora Caroline, he added, is very sensitive to bad smells, and Ricardo asked him how long he had known her. Since she become a widow three years before, the other answered. Ricardo thought he had misheard him. Señora Caroline is a widow? he asked. Señor Osvaldo died of cancer three years ago, the man said. Ricardo nodded, gave him a tip, and walked him to the door. After closing it, he stood there, motionless. He went back to his room to continue packing his suitcase, but he couldn't concentrate. He went to the kitchen to make a cup of coffee, which he drank on the balcony, asking himself why Caroline had lied to him. What prevented her from having him over or from her coming to his apartment? Was she afraid he would rape her? She was an old woman, thirty years older than him, if not more. For a moment he had the urge to knock on her chute hatch with the broomstick and ask for an explanation. But he felt hurt and decided he would leave the next day without saying goodbye.

It was later, when he woke from a brief nap, that he was struck by the memory of her way of sniffing her nightgown and arms when she thought he couldn't see her. He hadn't given it much thought, attributing it to the garbage chute, but on another occasion when he had caught her doing that, Caroline had blushed. Maybe she smelled bad, he told himself. Old people smell, not necessarily bad, but like old people. Or maybe it was something worse. He'd heard of a malodorous disease, which afflicted women more frequently than men. A friend of his mother's had had it. He went to his computer and searched the internet. The disease was called trimethylaminuria (TMAU) and was described as a condition that could be permanent or temporary, and the affected person was almost always the only one who did not perceive his bad smell, even if he smelled himself. He thought that maybe that was the reason why she didn't want to host him at her house or go to his; she had invented the story of the sick and jealous husband, and so he wouldn't notice the bad smell she was giving off, she'd suggested that they hold classes across the garbage chute, so it would act as a kind of shield.

While he was sitting in front of his computer, he had an idea and, as he tried to push it out of his mind, it created a pit in his stomach. He thought of the surprising way in which Marisa had left him, giving such vague reasons as their incompatibility; he thought of Villegas, who had canceled the trip to Melbourne with him; of Suárez himself, who had asked him to stay away because he had a cold, and of the sudden change of plans at the office, so that he would leave for Australia as soon as possible.

WILDLIFE CROSSING

As we know, wildlife crossings are constructions that allow animals to cross barriers built by humans, and as the need to preserve and respect wildlife has spread around the world, they have become more and more common. In most countries today, when a road, railroad line, or waterway is built through an area rich with animal life, a certain number of tunnels, viaducts, or bridges are designed along its length, which animals can cross without endangering their lives.

As the vast majority of wildlife crossings are not very long, animals cross them without any difficulty, and when there is a tunnel, they always have its end in sight, so they can venture into it without worrying about any danger. But this rule no longer applies to the large Musina Wildlife Crossing, located below the airport with the same name in South Africa. For political reasons, Musina Airport was built on the border between South Africa and Zimbabwe, adjacent to the Great Limpopo Transfrontier Park, which is one of the largest and most diverse wildlife sanctuaries in southern Africa. Elephants, zebras, wildebeests, and gazelles, as well as their respective predators, lions, leopards, hyenas, and cheetahs, cross the border between the two countries all the time inside the large preserve, in an area whose orographic characteristics force them to converge in a very narrow strip of terrain. Since most of the animals migrated through the terrain around the airport, a large wildlife corridor had to be built underneath it, as it became clear that animals should not be exposed to the constant takeoff and landing of airplanes. Because of its unusual length, more than eight hundred meters below ground, the main problem facing engineers and ecologists was how to allow large and small animals, situated at different places on the food chain, to travel unharmed through the almost kilometer-long underground passage. They concluded that the wildlife should be separated from each other, so the wildlife corridor was conceived as a wide network of tunnels.

Another problem was how to encourage the animals to venture into such an inhospitable environment. They needed a powerful incentive and someone came up with the idea that this might be a scent trail left by each species over its millenary transit through this place. It was decided, therefore, to expand that trail, along which odor pathways were projected by means of a series of subterranean tubes equipped with aromatizers that carry a particular scent into each tunnel in the wildlife passageway, which, depending on the need, is substituted by another one through an adjustable ventilation system. The scent of a pride of lions can be exchanged for that of a dazzle of zebras, and the latter for a troop of chimpanzees or a sounder of wild boars. Once an animal, or a group of animals, enters the wildlife corridor attracted by a particular odor, the system persuades or, conversely, discourages it from taking one tunnel rather than another. In other words, the animal is "guided" to the exit along an olfactory path that prevents it from "colliding" with animals that might pose a danger to it, such as a lion for a zebra, or a male lion for another male lion, or a dominant gorilla for another dominant gorilla.

All this, of course, requires a sophisticated camera system and constant monitoring. It's not surprising that the control room, from where the most suitable route is established for each animal, has more operators than the control tower of the airport itself, which is located above the wildlife crossing. All this is explained by the fact that aircraft follow human instructions blindly, while animals behave unpredictably. The fact that wildlife corridor operators are working only a few feet away from their aeronautical colleagues and that both groups are ultimately dealing with the same thing, which is controlling the reins of very problematic movements, such as returning a multiton device floating in the air to the ground and returning a distressed wild animal to its familiar habitat, has resulted in similar language use by the two groups; in other words, it is common for wildlife corridor operators to refer to the entry and exit of animals with phrases such as "Three gazelles landing safely in tunnel F14" or "Successful takeoff of male hyena in tunnel G3."

The construction of such an extensive wildlife crossing, in which the animals have no exit in sight and are forced to move forward guided only by their instincts, has created several problems. I'm going to focus on the two most important ones. The first is that you cannot use the same path to move in both directions. A herd of buffalo meeting another herd of buffalo coming the other way in a tunnel would be as catastrophic as the midair, head-on collision of two jumbo jets. It was therefore necessary to build not one but two separate tunnel systems, one for crossing from south to north, which was marked red, and the other for crossing the other way, which was marked green. Even so, the problem arose that an animal crossing from south to north, i.e., using the red route, will tend to use the same route on its return, because it's already familiar territory, and will ignore the green one. Therefore, it must be compelled to change its mind. To this end, it was proposed to "route" the animals to the correct entrance through a complex system of ditches, fences, and human patrols; but, besides being very expensive and risky, this procedure didn't guarantee complete success. The amazingly simple and inexpensive solution was provided by a hunter from the nearby nomadic Oungu tribe. The man asked engineers to dig a pit five feet deep and two feet wide at the outlet of both routes. He explained his idea. These pits located at the outlet of both routes would represent an obstacle for all animals; however, they would not represent the same kind of obstacle for animals coming from the tunnels as for those entering from the wild. No animal likes to jump, not even those that are particularly gifted at jumping, such as gazelles and leopards; they prefer to go around an obstacle rather than attempt to leap over it. Faced with a ditch standing between them and their natural habitat, the animals coming from the tunnels would hesitate a little, but with the urge to get back out into the open air, the ditch wouldn't be an insurmountable obstacle and after a brief hesitation they would overcome their fear and with certain determination jump or, in the case of heavy animals such as elephants, hippopotamuses, and rhinoceroses, step into and then walk out of the ditch. However, on the way back, the animals would come from the wild, not from the tunnels, and their mental state would be different. The red route ditch would cause them a more acute discomfort and they wouldn't be so willing to cross it at any cost, having to one side the clear entrance to the green route, so they would, without hesitating, opt for the latter.

The facts proved the hunter right. In fact, a simple ditch at the exit of the two tunnel networks was enough for all the animals, without exception, to use an outbound and an inbound route, just as the builders wanted.

The other problem that arose after the completion of the great Musina Wildlife Crossing was thornier, and in fact has yet to be solved. Because of its size and the relatively cool temperature of the tunnels, which is more pleasant than outside, there was a risk that some animals might make the wildlife corridor their home. To avoid this possibility, the tunnel was designed to offer no areas for rest, so that the animals would be forced to walk through it in one go. All of the tunnels have double exits, so there are no blind tunnels that could be mistaken for a cave. However, there is one tunnel that does not follow this rule, the one that connects the two tunnel systems, the red and the green. It's a very short passage, located at the center of the wildlife corridor, and was designed to link the two networks in case of an emergency. To keep animals out, its two entrances are so narrow that an adult zebra or gazelle would be unable to pass through them. Some, however, feared that a leopard might be able to get inside. A solitary animal by nature, its size would allow it to slip inside to turn the tunnel into a dwelling, from which it could, able to peer into both networks of tunnels, capture its prey; others objected that the leopard is an arboreal feline par excellence, which likes to perch on the branches of the acacias, where it feels safe from the attacks of larger predators, and have the vantage point from which it can see its hunting territory; it descends to the ground only to hunt and then returns with its prey to the safety of a perch. According to them, therefore, it was not likely that such an animal would want to remain in a subterranean chamber. Indeed, no leopard has entered the connecting tunnel. An old, wounded lion did, however, which was a possibility that no one had considered. When a male lion who leads a pride is driven out by another, stronger or younger lion, an agonizing ordeal begins for him that quickly ends in death; seriously wounded by the battle against the invading lion and unable to hunt large prey, he devotes himself to catching rabbits and mice, but these also escape him with ease; hungry and debilitated, he tends to hide so as not to be hunted in turn by hyenas and wild dogs; in the course of a few weeks he loses weight and musculature until he is reduced to mere skin and bones, and ends up dying in the bushes or on the edge of some watering hole or puddle where he comes to drink. It was this kind of lion that entered the connecting tunnel, slipping into it thanks to his extreme emaciation and probably intending to die there. But once inside that cool, damp chamber he must have recovered from his injuries, which were perhaps not so serious. Leaning out of one of the tunnels, he captured a baby gazelle that was passing by with its mother. He probably fine-tuned this hunting technique, the only one at his disposal, and to quench his thirst he must have learned to lick the moisture that dripped down the tunnel rock face. All this is pure conjecture, since there are no surveillance cameras in the connecting passageway. The only times that Johnny, as the wildlife corridor operators have christened the old lion, can be seen is when he peers into the tunnel to catch gazelle fawns, animals that make up his entire diet, since their tiny, sleek bodies are the only ones that he can drag into his den. As to the mystery of how he manages to traverse the two crossing entrances, his size being considerably larger than that of a leopard, one can only surmise that he must have learned to maintain a frugal diet, otherwise befitting his age, preserving himself in a state of sufficient thinness to enable him, surely not without some effort, to get his body through that space. In any case, Johnny has become the only permanent inhabitant of the Musina Wildlife Crossing.

When the Animal Protection Society accused the wildlife crossing authorities of sacrificing innocent victims for the old lion's diet, it was explained to them that taking Johnny out of that sort of cell where he himself had locked himself up would have been not only difficult but also counterproductive for the animals, since it would have forced them to close the complex for two or three days, with serious consequences for all of them, since they had already learned to use Musina as the most expeditious crossing to and from the Great Limpopo Park. But small gazelles have an allure that is hard to resist. So, predictably, public opinion has been polarized: those who advocate for Johnny and those who consider him a sneaky murderer. T-shirts with his photo, either to support or to vilify him, are sold by the thousands, and national and foreign tourists flock to Musina Airport not to board a plane but to watch the crossing of the beasts that takes place beneath the airport, in the hope of seeing Johnny's claw appear on the network of surveillance cameras in the wildlife corridor when he catches a baby gazelle. For a sector of society, especially women and young people, Johnny is nothing more than a parasite and represents the embodiment of the many ills that afflict the country, from the corruption of politicians to the spread of organized crime. Older people, however, see things differently. Separated from his herd, never able to see the light of day, and forced to make enormous efforts to slither into the only spot where he can access a bit of food, Johnny has become for many old people the spitting image of their hardship and they have made him the icon of their struggle for better living conditions. A national referendum has just been announced to decide the fate of the old lion: put him down with a lethal dart or let him live to continue feeding on newborn gazelles. Needless to say, philosophers, scientists, lawyers, politicians, artists, priests, and ordinary men and women are flooding the media every day with their opinions and arguments on this issue. Johnny, unaware of the fuss he has caused, is seen only for a few seconds each week, when he reaches his claw out to snatch a fawn from a mother gazelle, and lies in his den leading an almost monastic life. No one, since he has taken up residence in the central passageway of the Musina Wildlife Crossing, has heard him emit a single roar.

THE SADNESS OF TRANSLATION

I had just dropped out of an undergraduate program in sociology, despite my excellent record of academic performance. It was probably influenced by the fact that the university campus I was assigned to was an hour away by bus ride. I had to get up at five thirty every morning, when it was still dark outside, to get to class on time. The bus was full of bricklayers and construction workers nodding in and out of sleep. By the time I arrived at the school the sun was coming up. That lifestyle lasted a year, I got excellent grades, and suddenly I knew that I didn't care about anything I was learning. I couldn't think of anything else to do but start translating Italian poetry and hide the fact that I'd dropped out of college from my parents. They saw me getting up early to work in my room and when they thought it was strange that I wasn't attending classes, I told them that the subjects I was taking that semester allowed me to do my work at home and, because I was such an excellent student, I only had to take the exams. Their blind faith in my intellectual aptitudes, which I'd had since childhood, was satisfied by such an explanation and they never questioned me again.

I got up at five thirty every morning, the same time as when I went to university, but now it was to translate Ungaretti, Saba, and Pavese, and I couldn't stop thinking about the construction workers and bricklayers, crowded together on the bus, who for an entire year had shared so many trips with me in the dark.

Before long I realized that translating poetry was an impossible task. I doubted every word, even the simplest ones, like "dog" and "house." A "dog" wasn't the same in one language as in another; "house" in one language didn't evoke the same houses it evoked in another. Once finished, my translation was a clumsy replica of the poem I was trying to bring to life in another language. I became more and more convinced that translating was an outright hoax. Why was I doing it? Because I had nothing better to do and because other people had done it before me and were still doing it. I also thought that when we pronounce "casa" and "perro," we don't know if the person we are talking to understands the same thing as we do with those words. In short, the hoax was a deception that resulted from the language itself.

I struggled in particular with a very short poem by Ungaretti entitled "Soldiers":

Si sta
come d'autunno sugli alberi
le foglie.

My version went like this: "We exist / like in autumn / in the trees / the leaves."

It's a poem written during the First World War by the private Ungaretti, who sees how his trench mates are dying, just as autumn leaves dry on the trees. For that reason I translated the impersonal form *Si sta* as "We exist," because the poet speaks on behalf of his comrades; he includes himself as one more of the soldiers who at any moment can be struck down by a burst of shrapnel. However, Ungaretti, who could have used "we," did not. He did not write *Stiamo*, but *Si sta*. The problem was that in Spanish the "Se existe" sounded too forced, far from the naturalness of the Italian *Si sta*. Why? I don't know. Every language, like any living being, has its temperament, its inclinations, and its preferences. Do you understand me now when I say that poetry is untranslatable? That short, clear, and perfectly formed poem, when translated, leaks all over the place.

I had a girlfriend at the time, my first true love. She was the only one who knew that I had abandoned the degree I was pursuing. It was our secret. She was worried about me dropping out and when she asked if it was a temporary or permanent withdrawal, I realized that she was thinking about the idea of marrying me and wondering how we were going to support ourselves. I just hugged her and kissed her. My days were reduced to loving her and translating Italian poetry. I was being supported by my parents, who were still unaware of the fact that I'd dropped out of school. When I ask myself why that Ungaretti poem haunted me, I think that perhaps I saw it as a test of my abilities as a translator and, by extension, as an aspiring writer. If I failed to translate such a clear little poem, it meant I had to give up writing. I later learned that such clear little poems are the most difficult to translate, but I didn't know that at the time.

I fought so bitterly with that poem because I identified with it. I was also at an extremely precarious moment in my life, holding on as a leaf holds on to a branch.

One day a miracle happened. Flipping through the pages of a literary supplement, I found the translations of several Ungaretti poems, among them "Soldiers." According to a footnote, the translator was a Latin professor from our distinguished national university. My chest swelled with emotion. I'd forgotten that there were other translators out there. The same poem that had caused me so much frustration was right here. The professor had chosen neither the form "Se está" nor the form "Estamos" but an intermediate form, "Se está uno," which I had rejected as a crude solution. It solved the problem, but in a perfunctory way. However, I decided to call him and ask if I could meet him, thinking that perhaps the man would be interested in meeting a young colleague who translated the same poet as he did. I spoke to the literary supplement editorial staff and they didn't hesitate at all to give me his telephone number. He answered kindly and showed interest in my translations, but when I proposed to meet him, he told me he was extremely busy. His voice was muffled, as if he'd just woken up. I insisted a bit and he gave in: we could have coffee the next day at a café near his house. Cecilia, my girlfriend, asked me if she could come with me. I would have preferred to go alone, because going on my first literary date with my girlfriend seemed inappropriate, but then I thought that Cecilia, with her cheerfulness and easy laugh, would be a blessing in case the interview with the professor turned sour.

When we arrived, the man was sitting at a table with a cup of coffee in front of him. He guessed who we were just by seeing us walk in and waved us over. He wasn't the haggard old man I had imagined listening to him on the phone. As soon as he saw us he noticed Cecilia's legs and immediately pushed back a lock of hair that covered his forehead. He seemed to be about fifty years old. His hair was long, and maybe he wore it that way so as not to trim that lock, which he lifted several times in what seemed to be a carefully practiced movement during our conversation. Cecilia had dressed the way I liked best, in black stockings, a plaid skirt, and a low-cut blouse that accentuated that naughty girlish look that made me fall in love with her from the first moment I saw her. The man stood up to greet us and, since it was a booth, he gave Cecilia the place next to the window, inviting me to sit next to her, but since that meant moving his coffee cup, I thought it would be polite to leave him where he was, that is, next to Cecilia, and I would occupy the seat in front of him. It was an unusual situation, but I didn't think anything of it. I had several translations of Ungaretti with me, which I showed him. He was patient and cordial, gave them moderate praise, and told me that perhaps he could get them published in the same supplement where he had published his or in another whose editor was his best friend. I blushed with pleasure and thanked him. He urged me to keep working, but it was clear that all his attention was directed at Cecilia, whose bare arms he kept staring at.

At some point I left to go to the bathroom. When I returned, he was stroking her arm, but when he saw me he quickly pulled his hand away. I felt the gut punch and I had the absurd thought that Cecilia and the professor knew each other. I told them that I'd forgotten something and went back to the bathroom, where I stood in front of the sinks for about five minutes, looking at myself in the mirror, not knowing what to do. I felt like a coward for not saying anything and, knowing Cecilia, I sensed that she was as confused as I was, but I couldn't believe she hadn't mustered the courage to pull her arm away. When I went back to the table, the teacher was gone. Cecilia told me that he had left without explanation, after paying the bill. I sat down in the place he had occupied and said, without looking at her:

"He was caressing your arm. Why?"

I'd hoped that she would give me a convincing explanation.

"He told me that I had beautiful arms. I thanked him and he asked me for my permission to caress them."

"And why'd you let him?"

She shrugged her shoulders. "He was so kind to you that I didn't want to tell him no. And you, why'd you go back to the bathroom?"

"I left my watch when I took it off to wash my hands." She grabbed her pack of cigarettes, took one out, and lit it, looking out the window. I asked her what the professor had said to her before he left. She took another puff, turned to me, and calmly replied, "He said that your translations are worthless." She looked back outside.

"And did he say why?" My voice trembled as I asked her.

"No, he just said that and left."

"What a rotten person. And you believe him?"

She shook her head.

"You're hesitating," I said. "He made you second-guess them."

I expected her to say something like "If that guy thinks your translations are worthless, he's an asshole"; instead she was silent and that indifference of hers scared the hell out of me. One sentence from the professor had been enough to dethrone me from the pedestal she had put me on. Or maybe she'd never had me on a pedestal to begin with. When I looked at her I resented her and noticed her arm resting on the table in the same position as before, as if she was longing for the man's caresses. I stood up and told her we should leave. She took it in stride, took two more puffs on her cigarette and crushed the butt in the ashtray, stood up, and walked toward the exit with a poise I'd never known her to have.

We didn't see or speak to each other for a week. It wasn't the first time such a thing had happened, but I had a feeling that this time it was different. Every minute of that prolonged silence confirmed to me that Cecilia had changed. What had the professor said to her while stroking her arm, besides the fact that my translations were worthless? When I finally spoke to her to find out, she answered from the airport, where she was about to board a plane with her parents. They were going on vacation, to San Antonio; I was so surprised that I didn't even ask her when she was coming back. It was the first time she'd ever gone on a trip without telling me. I didn't ask her anything, I didn't mention the professor, and after I ended the call I was left thinking that the Cecilia I loved no longer existed.

A few days later my mother asked me why Cecilia hadn't been coming to the house, and when I told her that we'd stopped seeing each other, her mouth gaped open but she didn't say a word. She and Papá adored her.

In the days that followed I noticed the effort they made not to ask me if I'd spoken to her. I could hear them whispering all the time. It was an agonizing few days. Luckily, two old schoolmates I hadn't seen for a long time, Osvaldo and Felipe, invited me to spend a week with them at the beach. The excursion was a huge relief, and yet during the whole trip I couldn't help sensing from my two friends a certain attitude of restraint and condescension toward me, similar to the one my parents had since I'd told them that Cecilia and I were no longer dating. Were they aware of the same thing, even though they'd never met Cecilia?

On my way back from the beach, giving in to a sudden impulse, I called the professor. I was retranslating

Ungaretti's poems for the umpteenth time and decided to call him and invite him for a coffee. I didn't know why I wanted to see him, let alone what I was going to say to him, but I had a phrase I could use to my advantage: "You left the last time without saying goodbye." When he answered it was the first thing I said to him, and the phrase had an effect, because he asked me about my translations. He agreed to have coffee with me and arranged to meet me at another coffee shop near his house the following afternoon. He didn't show the slightest hint of surprise or disappointment when he saw me arrive without Cecilia, or he knew how to hide it. I was tanned from the beach and he wanted to know where I'd gone. He talked for a while about the beaches on the Pacific he was familiar with. I'd pegged him as a bookworm and learned that he was a passionate lover of the sea, a regular camper, and a good swimmer. He recommended several off-the-beaten-path beaches and that's where most of our conversation went. I had to admit that he was a nice man. Suddenly he dropped the maritime topic and asked me what I thought of his Ungaretti translations. I couldn't help blushing, because I'd reread them before our appointment and they still seemed mediocre. He must have guessed, because he said:

"You know Ungaretti much better than I do. Speak your mind."

I told him what I thought. He'd wrapped Ungaretti's luminous dryness in a colloquial tone that reduced his poems to polite vignettes. He'd coated them in a veneer, caressed them to the point of numbness.

For a moment I was afraid he was going to say, "Just like I caressed your girlfriend's arm?" Instead, he said that maybe I was right, and I realized that my literary dictum had impressed him. Up to that point he had been conducting the conversation, pleased to see me nod at almost everything he said, and all at once I'd shown him that I was capable of doing more than nodding my head. He asked me what I did for a living. He hadn't asked me at our previous meeting, and realizing that made me see how little he had been interested in me, captivated as he was by Cecilia's good looks. I replied that I'd abandoned my sociology studies to concentrate on translating Italian poetry. It was an outlandish answer, to say the least, and I felt obliged to clarify that I was being supported by my parents for the time being. He asked me why I hadn't enrolled in classical languages. Latin and Greek, he said, were invaluable tools for any translator. He had gone back to leading the conversation, and I was nodding my head again. Suddenly he looked at his watch and said he had to leave. We asked for the bill. Outside the café, as we shook hands, he asked me to say hello to my girlfriend for him.

"She's not my girlfriend anymore."

He merely nodded, and I, still squeezing his hand, told him point-blank:

"She told me that you thought my translations were no good."

He let go of my hand, incredulous:

"Absolutely not! She asked me what I thought of them, and I answered that they were very good, although I wasn't completely convinced by all of them."

"She asked you what you thought of them?"

"Yes, and if it was possible to make a living as a translator. I told her no, obviously." I wondered if he hadn't stroked her arm to comfort her after seeing her heartbroken expression at that answer. Evidently, Cecilia feared that I wouldn't be able to support myself translating poetry. I didn't say anything and he thought he should give me an explanation as to why my translations were not to his liking:

"They're too spare. Italian is your mother tongue and you understand Ungaretti better than I do, but you dehydrate him too much. A little kindness, which I have plenty of, wouldn't do you any harm."

I was about to ask him if it was that kindness that he had so much of that had led him to caress Cecilia's arm. Instead, I said that had Ungaretti not died and had he been there with us, we would have asked him which style of translation he preferred, the spare one or the kind one. He laughed out loud, which gave me a glimpse of the man who loves to go camping and the expert swimmer hidden beneath the surface of the dour Latin professor. I hope we can do this again, he said. We exchanged cell phone numbers and he said goodbye, shaking my hand warmly.

Why had Cecilia asked him if he liked my translations, when the professor had already approved them, even offering to publish them in the same literary supplement where he had published his own? Had she asked him when he started stroking her arm, to distract him with that question and prevent him from going overboard, or because she sincerely doubted my ability? Now more than ever that gesture haunted me; I'd broken it down trying to guess my girlfriend's feelings, and I realized that I'd met with the professor once again because I'd hoped to discover them by talking to him. But our conversation had gone in a different direction, and I would have looked like a jealous idiot if I'd brought up the subject to demand an explanation.

That afternoon when I had been denied one revelation, I was offered another that I wasn't even close to imagining. While I was walking away after saying goodbye to the professor, I saw Arizmendi, an old schoolmate I hadn't seen for a couple of years, coming toward me. Although we'd never been close friends, we liked each other and I was glad to see him. He had a kind of spastic tic on his right side, but he carried that defect very well; it was noticeable only when I shook his right hand, which, when he offered to shake mine, felt like a soft, lifeless glove. He told me that he had heard about my trip to the beach with Felipe and Osvaldo, after I had broken up with my girlfriend. I asked him who had told him that I'd broken up with my girlfriend and he said Felipe and Osvaldo. I hadn't said a single word to them about Cecilia, I was sure of that; they didn't even know her. Seeing that I didn't respond, Arizmendi must have felt that he'd said something he should have kept to himself and, claiming that he was late for an appointment, he wished me well and said goodbye. I watched him walk away in his unbalanced gait, while I wondered how Osvaldo and Felipe knew about my relationship with Cecilia. There were only two people who could have told him about her, and they were my parents. I saw my mother's anguished face again when I'd told her that Cecilia and I had split up. Osvaldo and Felipe's invitation to join them at the beach had saved me from the somber atmosphere that had fallen over my house from the moment I'd mentioned it to them. Felipe had called my house, and because I wasn't home, he'd spoken to my mother, and it had been she who had filled me in on the details of the trip, from the name of the beach to the bungalows where we were going to stay, and it had seemed strange to me that my friend had gone into so much detail with her before talking to me. The invitation itself was strange, because Osvaldo and Felipe belonged to my group of friends, but our relationship had always been superficial. As Arizmendi's silhouette got lost in the distance, I knew that my parents had organized that trip to help me out of the bad moment I was going through. They'd asked Osvaldo and Felipe to invite me to the beach, in exchange for paying for everything, and that's how my two friends knew about my breakup with Cecilia. But there had to be something else for my parents to have taken on that expense, and that could only be my decision to drop out of college. Cecilia, who was the only one who knew about it, had told them at some point, betraying our secret, because she was sure I was doing something stupid. That's why she had misrepresented the professor's judgment about my translations, hoping that this would make me reconsider my decision to abandon my studies, which made her see little promise for her future with me. She had hoped that my disappointment would make me come to my senses and get back on the right track. I was standing in the middle of the sidewalk, detached from the street noise and the people passing by, transported back to that afternoon with my girlfriend and the professor, and I suddenly saw Cecilia reach her arm across the table for him to caress it. I wondered if she had asked him explicitly or if it had been enough for her to let it fall on the table with that naughty girlish smile that had made me fall in love with her from the first moment I'd seen her. And he, had he guessed the intention of that gesture of hers, with which she intended to nip my literary whims in the bud?

I took out my cell phone and dialed his number.

"Hola, Luis," he said when he answered, and it was the first time he had called me by my name.

For a moment I was tempted to tell him that I had the wrong number, hang up, and never see him again; I saw myself at home tearing up my Ungaretti translations and the next day I would go back to studying sociology, and when Cecilia returned from San Antonio, I'd talk to her about my decision, which would bring her back into my arms. But the professor had said my name and I knew it was necessary to confront him.

"I wanted to ask you something I didn't have the nerve to ask you at the café," I said. "It's something I'm stuck on."

"I'm listening."

I cleared my throat. I wanted my voice to sound calm. I asked him if, when he had started translating poetry, he hadn't felt like an impostor; that simple words like "dog" and "house" couldn't be translated as they were, because they meant something different in every language.

He remained silent for a brief moment before answering me:

"Of course I've felt that way. All translators wonder at one point or another if we aren't impostors, Luis, you can rest assured."

LETTERS TO THE QUEEN

The prince phoned around lunchtime. He introduced himself by giving his title, followed by his first and last name, added that he was the son-in-law of the queen of Italy, and then he asked to speak to Rubén. She passed the phone to her son. Rubén and the prince spoke for less than a minute and when her son hung up, she hadn't moved, anxious to know why the queen's son-in-law had wanted to talk to him.

"He's coming over this afternoon from C. to give me one of his letters that he wants me to translate into Italian," Rubén said. "It's for the queen."

"For the queen?" She pressed her hand to her chest. "Will you be able to do it?"

"He told me it's a simple letter. He's Argentinean, he can't write in Italian, and that's why he wants me to translate it for him."

"And how does he know about you?"

"They gave him our number at the embassy."

When they sat down to eat, she told Rubén that there was a nice tea service on sale at the Palacio de Hierro. If she hurried, she could go and buy it before the prince arrived. But she decided not to. It was late and she still had to change, because she wasn't going to receive the prince dressed in her everyday clothes. She went to her bedroom and picked out a dress with a floral print and a wide neckline that made her look younger; she changed her house slippers for open-toed shoes with heels that she had worn to the wedding of her friend Cecilia's daughter, and spent half an hour applying her makeup. When she came out of her room, Rubén, seeing her so well dressed, asked her where she was going, and she replied that it wasn't every day that one received a visit from a member of the royal family.

The prince arrived punctually. He wore a beige linen suit that highlighted his tan, a plaid shirt, and suede loafers. He was a tall, slightly stooped man, and Rubén was surprised by the size of his feet. The man kissed his mother's hand, which made her blush a little. She offered him coffee, and, as she went to the kitchen to prepare it, he took an envelope out of his briefcase and removed a sheet of paper from it, which he then handed to Rubén. It was the letter addressed to the queen, and Rubén read through it immediately. It was handwritten, in small but perfectly legible script, and it spoke only of Lucas, the prince's son, who had just turned four. After the description of the birthday party, the prince listed the new words Lucas had learned, recounted a couple of funny things the boy had done, and, in conclusion, told the queen that the boy was taking swimming lessons in the house pool, the exact temperature of the water also included. The prince asked him if he understood his handwriting; Rubén replied that it was very clear and told him that he could translate the letter right away. The prince thanked him profusely. He went to his room, sat down at the table, and got to work. As he translated, he heard his mother telling the prince how hard she had struggled to teach her only son to speak Italian, a struggle that had earned her the enmity of her husband's family and, eventually, a divorce. Now, at sixteen, Rubén was more fluent in Italian than she was.

"A mother should pass her own language on to her child, at any cost," she said, and the prince agreed with her.

When he had finished translating the letter, Rubén went back to the living room and handed it to the prince, who read it and said it was perfect. He pointed out that when he informed the queen of little Lucas's progress he hadn't specified what progress he was referring to, so the sentence was somewhat ambiguous. The prince reread the sentence, agreed that it was unclear, and asked him what he recommended he should include.

"I think you're referring to his swimming progress," Rubén said, and the prince nodded vigorously. That was what he had wanted to say and asked him if he could add that.

"I'll bring you the pen," his mother said, and she hurried to her son's room and brought the pen, and he sat down at the living room table and amended the sentence. The prince asked him if he could add something that would give a little color to the matter, some funny detail so that the queen would have a better idea of who her grandson was. Rubén thought about it for a moment and said:

"You can say that Lucas already knows how to put his head underwater and hold his breath."

"Fantastic!"

While Rubén added that sentence, the prince told his mother that one afternoon on Lake Como, walking along the shores of the lake in the company of his mother-in-law, that is, the queen, people recognized the latter and a large group of people immediately gathered to show their admiration and affection, a clear sign, according to him, of how much the Italians missed the royal house that had ruled them for more than a century. His mother nodded in approval:

"A queen is a queen!"

Rubén read the sentence to them in Italian so they could hear how it had turned out:

"Lucas already knows how to open his eyes underwater and waves his little hands around while blowing bubbles out of his mouth."

"Excellent!" the prince exclaimed, and his mother, who was beside herself with delight, offered him another cup of coffee. The prince declined her offer and folded the letter to put it in his briefcase, but hesitated for a moment and asked Rubén if he wouldn't mind writing another letter to the queen, in which he would report on more of Lucas's progress. He would send Jonás, his chauffeur, for it that weekend.

She answered for her son:

"Rubén would love to write another letter to the queen."

The prince explained that his wife knew nothing of this correspondence between the queen and himself. Mother and daughter didn't see eye to eye, and he had decided to write to the queen to update her on the health of her grandson. He had tried to write the letter himself, but his written Italian was very bad, so he had contacted the embassy and asked for someone who could translate a private letter into Italian quickly. He had been given the names of three people, two ladies employed by the embassy and Rubén. When he was told that he was a sixteen-year-old boy, he had immediately preferred him to the two ladies. Then he added:

"If you can share something funny it would be wonderful. The queen loves amusing events and anecdotes."

"Like what?" Rubén asked.

The prince told him that he could make Jonás, the chauffeur, who was a fat man, fall into the pool, and as he said that he laughed as if he were actually seeing the man splashing about. Rubén asked if he wanted him to add that clumsy tumble to the same letter or in another one.

"If it could be all at once in this one, that would be marvelous," the prince said.

His mother intervened:

"You'll do a great job, son."

Rubén took the letter from the prince's hands and went to his room, leaving the door open. He heard his mother ask the prince if he would like a glass of port while they waited for him to finish the letter, and the prince replied that he would gladly have one.

The addition of a comic incident forced him to rewrite the letter from scratch. He had no trouble plunging Jonás into the water because of a slip on the edge of the pool. He thought of inserting a banana peel as the cause behind the fall, but thought it was a rather crude technique. Finally, while half listening to the conversation between his mother and the prince (she was telling him that on her mother's side she was of Piedmontese blood, just like the Italian royal house), he decided that the chauffeur would stumble for no specific reason and, to make the incident more colorful, he made little Lucas, who at the time was treading water in his floaty toy, laugh out loud. The prince was telling his mother that he was surprised that a beautiful woman like her hadn't remarried after the divorce, to which she replied, lowering her voice in a confidential tone, that taking care of her son was the most important concern she had. Rubén heard them clink their glasses and after that they were silent. That pause in the conversation grew longer and longer and he stopped writing so he could concentrate on it. The silence became increasingly ominous and even if he only had to stand up and peek out the door to see what the prince and his mother were doing, his trepidation kept him stuck to his chair. He tried to catch some indication that would confirm his fears, such as a gasp or their clothes rustling together. Even if nothing was happening, he considered it scandalous, because it gave rise to suspicion, and he hated his mother, who apparently still thought of him as a child and thus it didn't cross her mind that he might interpret this silence in the worst way. He heard the prince's voice ask something, and her voice was soft when she answered him. So it was true, something despicable had just happened and now they were speaking in whispers so he wouldn't hear them. There, in their apartment, while he was in his room! Had the world gone crazy? Or had his mother and the prince known each other before? The conversation between them returned to the tone and loquacity of a few minutes before, and the abruptness of this change seemed to him proof that they had just committed some inappropriate act. He struggled to finish the letter and as he left the desk he cleared his throat to warn them that he was done, and he returned to the living room.

The prince smiled as he read the letter and gave it to Rubén's mother to read, but not before telling her that her son was going to be a great writer. She couldn't help but agree with him, seeing how well Rubén had described the driver's belly flop, how he first stumbled on the grass, stumbled over the cement edge of the pool, and fell into the water with a slap. She handed the letter back to the prince, who was silent for a few moments. The smile had disappeared from his face, and with the same seriousness with which he had prophesied to Rubén a brilliant destiny as a writer, he said, not without a slight blush:

"I think it would be fantastic if I fell into the water too, Rubén."

It was the first time he had said his name.

"You?" his mother asked.

"Yes, but in another letter, not this one. Jonás could pick it up this Saturday."

"You want me to make you fall in the water?" Rubén asked.

"Yes, like Jonás." His face was flushed.

"Fall in completely, and with a belly flop?"

"Completely and with a belly flop. The queen will love it." Rubén looked at his mother, seeking her approval.

"It will turn out perfectly," she said.

The prince put the letter in his briefcase and stood up, followed by Rubén's mother, whose hand he kissed. As he gave Rubén's hand a warm squeeze, he again told him that he had no doubt he would be a writer, and earnestly requested that he finish the letter by the following Saturday.

His mother walked the prince to the door. After closing the door, she hugged Rubén.

"Did you hear that? You're going to be a great writer!"

He didn't return her embrace and she pulled away, puzzled. She asked him what was bothering him.

"Did he kiss you?"

She was furious:

"What are you talking about?"

"The two of you stopped talking while I was in my room! What were you doing?"

Her expression was incredulous but then she understood:

"He took out his checkbook and made out a check to me, that's why we stopped talking. Look." She went to the table in the middle of the room, where there was a check, picked it up, and showed it to him.

Rubén looked at the check.

"How could you think that?" She approached him and hugged him again. That night, when he went to bed, he was unable to fall asleep, because the disturbing excitement he'd felt in his room while his mother and the prince were silent was still floating around in his head. All he had to do was remember those moments to relive the agitation that had frozen him in his chair. He thought that, even if nothing had happened, his mother should have come to his room to ask him how the letter was going. If she hadn't done so, staying by the prince's side while he drew up the check instead, wasn't it because she'd wanted him to kiss her?

Hadn't she spent almost an hour getting ready?

The next afternoon, opening one of the kitchen cabinets, he discovered a new tea set and asked his mother when she'd bought it. She replied that she'd bought it that very morning, because it was on sale at the palace.

"Why'd you buy it? The chauffeur's the one coming on Saturday, not the prince."

"I didn't buy it for the prince," she replied. "Haven't you seen how all our dishes are chipped?"

On Saturday Rubén went to his soccer match, and when she was alone, she put on her new dress, a dark blue linen ensemble with a plunging neckline, which she'd also bought at the palace along with the tea set. She put on the open-toed shoes she'd worn the first time and applied her makeup carefully. When the intercom buzzed, her heart almost leapt out of her chest, but as she lifted the receiver she felt a sharp disappointment. It was the chauffeur, not the prince. She hadn't given up hope that he would change his mind and come to pick up the new letter personally. She could see herself offering him tea in the brand-new service she'd purchased at the palace while he told her anecdotes about the queen and his wife, the princess.

The chauffeur was a small, fat man, his hair was cut short, and he wore a dark suit and was panting from having climbed the stairs.

"Jonás Jiménez, at your service. The elevator is out of order, isn't it?"

"It breaks down all the time."

She felt ridiculous for having spent almost an hour making herself up for that man. She told him she was Rubén's mother and to sit down while she went to get the letter. The other, instead of sitting down, asked her about her son. She told him he wasn't there.

"You see..." He was still panting and he hesitated, searching for the words. "The prince wanted to ask your son, if it's at all possible, if he could change the letter a little."

"Change it how?"

"You see... he came to the conclusion that it's not appropriate... that it's not appropriate for him to fall into the water."

"But he was the one who asked Rubén to write that."

"Yes, but he thought it over and came to the conclusion that it's better for me to fall in."

"Again? You fell in already in the first letter!"

The driver looked surprised: "I fell into the water?"

"Yes, you did a belly flop. Didn't the prince tell you?"

"No."

"Anyway, Rubén isn't here, he went to play soccer."

The other pursed his lips: "I understand, but you...by any chance could you do it?"

"Do what?"

"Make the change between me and the prince. You're Italian, aren't you?"

"Yes, of Piedmontese blood."

"You see, the prince needs the letter right away. We're going to the Italian embassy as soon as we leave here. The prince wants to take advantage of the fact that the diplomatic pouch is leaving today to send the letter to the queen."

"You're going to the embassy? Is the prince with you?"

"He's in the car, waiting for me."

"Why didn't he come up?"

"He has some important calls to make and preferred to stay downstairs."

She felt a sudden, sharp pain. She'd bought a new dress to welcome the prince back into her home, and he hadn't even taken the trouble to come upstairs. The chauffeur looked at his watch:

"The pouch leaves at one o'clock. If you could..."

"I can't write to the queen of Italy, that's impossible," she exclaimed, a hint of anger in her voice.

"Try."

She felt the urge to rush at the man but restrained herself. She wasn't going to be rude. The prince was rude, wanting her son to change the letter and sending his chauffeur to tell him so, instead of asking him personally... He was the rude one! After all the compliments he had paid Rubén a few days before, what would it have cost him to come up for a moment? Nobles can be louts as much as anyone else, she thought to herself. But, on the face of it, the prince wasn't a nobleman; he wasn't even Italian. He was an upstart and all the compliments he'd paid Rubén were disingenuous.

The chauffeur said, in a conciliatory tone, "All you have to do, señora, is make a few changes to your son's letter, so that I am the one who falls into the water, instead of the prince."

"What's so funny about you falling in again? The queen won't find it funny, she'll just think you're a fool for falling into the water all the time."

The man, who had been smiling until then, stopped smiling completely. She went back to her point:

"Is that what you want? That the queen of Italy thinks you're a fool?"

The man had turned pale.

"Do you know the queen, Señor Jonás?"

"No, the queen has never come to Mexico, she will come this summer to meet her grandson."

"How would you like it if, when the queen comes and sees you, she says to herself: here's the fool who is tripping and falling into the pool all the time? The queen, Señor Jonás, the queen of Italy."

The chauffeur was astonished and looked at her without blinking. He was still breathing heavily from the six flights of stairs he had climbed. He asked her if he could sit down.

"Are you feeling okay?"

"No, I'm fine, I'm just short of breath, I climbed too fast." And without waiting for her permission, he sat down on the edge of the sofa. He touched his heart and she was afraid he was going to pass out.

"Are you sure you don't feel faint?"

"I'm sure."

"Would you like a glass of water?"

"If it wouldn't be too much trouble."

She went to the kitchen, filled a glass of water, and took it to him. The other thanked her and she stood there, uncomfortable. She decided to leave him alone and went to Rubén's room to get the letter. She would give it to the chauffeur as it was and let the prince do with it as he wished. It was on Rubén's desk, in an envelope he had taped shut. Her son hadn't shown it to her. Since the prince's visit, he had locked himself inside a kind of desperate silence. She had made a couple of attempts to soothe him and in the end had let him simmer in his brooding. Suddenly she felt the need to read the letter, opened the envelope, and took out the sheet of paper. It was very brief and when she finished reading it she felt faint. It was abysmally silly. The prince described his fall into the water, blaming it on the size of his feet, which were always playing tricks on him. Damn feet, he repeated three times.

There was nothing funny about it. On top of that, he was in his bathing suit, which made the stumble less dramatic, and no one had seen him fall into the water. It was a solitary incident that would leave the queen cold. She thought the prince would tear the letter to pieces after reading it. That was what she did and threw the pieces in the wastebasket. She wasn't going to allow the prince to read such a banal letter, after having told Rubén that he was going to be a writer. She peered into the living room, where the chauffeur was taking a sip from his glass of water.

"Since you insist, I'll see what I can do," she said.

"Thank you very much, señora."

She walked over to Rubén's desk, sat down, and rolled a sheet of paper onto the spool of the typewriter. She got up again and went to the living room to ask the chauffeur how deep the pool was at the prince's house. He told her that it was twelve feet deep at its deepest part.

"Do you know how to swim?"

The man hesitated, as if such a question couldn't be answered casually.

"To be honest, no, but once I wanted to—"

She didn't let him finish and returned to the desk with the idea of cutting the fall into the pool altogether. It was a clichéd device, unworthy of Rubén's talent. She decided that the prince would order Jonás to learn how to swim, for his own safety and the safety of Lucas himself. She stuffed the chauffeur into a large black life preserver made from a tire, next to the prince's son. The swimming instructor made them kick in the water, holding on to the edge of the pool, and the little four-year-old, who already had experience with this exercise, laughed his head off at all the grunts and groans of suffering from his fat companion, who was swallowing water because he had a hard time keeping his head above water. Then the instructor asked both of them to lower their heads, but to keep their eyes open under the water, and again Lucas erupted in laughter when he saw that Jonás immediately pulled his head out, bursting into exclamations of panic. The instructor had to go into the water to calm him down, while the driver put his hands to his eyes, which were burning like fire. She couldn't believe that the phrases of her native language were so easily strung together in her head. It was as if they had been lying dormant for so many years, waiting for the right moment to come to light, and now they flowed effortlessly, as if someone was dictating them to her. She found herself laughing as she typed on the machine and felt tenderness for the chunky, helpless man who barely fit inside the inner tube and was going through this ordeal to keep Lucas out of harm's way. The man, hearing her laugh, stood up, walked to where she was, and, standing by the door, asked her:

"Have you already made me fall into the water, señora?"

"Not quite," she answered without looking up, "but the queen will adore you when she finally meets you."

DAEDALUS UNDER BERLIN

Pencroff is one of a large contingent of GDR masons tunneling underground in East Berlin. Divided into six- or seven-man crews, they dig with pickaxes for eight hours a day, then shovel the earth into buckets, which they carry to the junction with a main tunnel and empty into wagons on rails that will carry it to the surface. It has to be done exclusively with picks, without the aid of jackhammers or any other noisy tools that might give away the existence of the tunnels to the West Berlin secret service. The masons have been told that it is a vast plan to renovate the city's sewage system, an explanation that fools no one, because if that were the case, it would be hard to understand why the work had to be done in secret.

Once the men go underground, they are taken in a wagon to the point where they are supposed to dig. There are watchmen walking through the tunnels supervising their work. Often the men in a crew hear voices on the other side of a tunnel wall and dig until the wall collapses, revealing yet another tunnel where yet more workers are digging. Thus, a rumor has arisen that a large subterranean labyrinth is being created under East Berlin that is intended to prevent people from escaping to the West. The idea is that anyone attempting to escape to the other side of the Wall through a tunnel will at some point run into this cramped network of galleries and become trapped in its endless spider's web.

Pencroff has befriended Ivan Zossimov, a young Russian member of his crew whose girlfriend, Katiusha, works as a secretary at the USSR embassy in East Berlin. According to Zossimov, Katiusha is privy to secrets unknown to the GDR authorities themselves, since the orders for the labyrinth have come directly from Moscow. When Pencroff tells Sabine, his young wife, she has no problem believing everything he tells her. She is obsessed with the labyrinth, she talks of nothing else, and when her husband returns from work she pesters him with questions to find out what other news his Russian friend has told him. In the factory where she works, there are rumors that since Gorbachev came to power, big changes are coming, changes in the direction the country is heading and in the USSR itself. That's why one day she tells her husband to invite Zossimov over for dinner because the Russian, due to his relationship with the Soviet embassy, must be aware of many things that they don't know about. Pencroff doesn't like to have people over to his apartment, so he acts as if he doesn't know anything, but Sabine insists that he ask Zossimov if he wants to come to dinner with his fiancée, and Pencroff finally gives in.

The Russian gladly accepts the invitation, and from the moment he walks into his home, Pencroff feels a sharp uneasiness. A jealous man, he discovers, when he opens the door, that Zossimov is a very attractive young man. Because of the dim light from the lamps in the tunnels, the masks that the members of the crews wear to protect themselves from the dust, and the helmets that cover their foreheads, he had seen only half of the Russian's face, and only now, when he opened the door of his apartment, did he notice how handsome he was. He feels as if he's going to faint. Sabine, who is fifteen years younger than him, is about the same age as the Russian. The latter, moreover, comes without his girlfriend, because Katiusha, he explains, woke up with a fever. In addition to being handsome, Zossimov shows himself to be possessed of the gift of conversational charm, which makes him the center of attention during the entire evening. Sabine has invited Karla, a colleague from the factory with whom she has become inseparable, and Pencroff is relegated to a second plane, or rather a third plane, since the second plane is occupied by Sabine and Karla, who hang on Zossimov's every word and bombard him with questions about the underground labyrinth, about Gorbachev, about the future of world communism, about how the women of his country dress, and countless other topics. During the entire evening the owner of the apartment feels as though he is worth less than a dried-up piece of shit, observing the rapt expression with which his wife keeps staring at his guest, and the next day, in the tunnels, the very sight of the young Russian produces such a violent aversion in him that he is unable to address a single friendly word to the man. Zossimov asks him what's bothering him, and he replies that he woke up with a terrible migraine. The other gives him a card with the name of a doctor at the Russian embassy, Kobeliev, who, for an unspecified amount of money, will write up a medical certificate that would allow him to be absent from work and even to obtain an indefinite leave of absence, just as Kobeliev did for one of his friends when he issued him a certificate stating that he was suffering from severe arthritis, a certificate his friend managed to use to be transferred from the assembly line where he worked to a desk in the accounting department. Pencroff thanks him and keeps the card.

The next day Sabine has one of the vertigo attacks she often suffers from and phones in that she won't be able to go to work. When Pencroff enters the tunnels and climbs into the wagon, he sees that Zossimov isn't there, asks about him, and is told that he called in sick. Pencroff suspects a secret meeting between Zossimov and his wife and struggles to keep himself from getting out of the wagon and running home. That delusion haunts him as he sinks his pickaxe into the ground. He works so hard that his coworkers make fun of him. One of them asks him if he's had a fight with his wife, the others laugh, and Pencroff interprets their laughter as proof that the crew is aware of the collusion between his wife and the young Russian. He lunges at the guy who uttered that phrase, and the others have to jump in to separate them. Over the next few hours they keep their distance from him, and no one says a word to him the rest of the day. Back home he finds Sabine recovered from her bout of vertigo and searches the apartment for any sign of Zossimov's presence. He finds nothing and asks Sabine if she went out, thinking that perhaps she and the Russian met somewhere else, to which she angrily responds by asking him how he thinks that with such a severe case of vertigo she could have thought of going out.

The next day in the tunnels, Pencroff asks Zossimov if he was really sick, and the Russian, as he had suspected, replies that he was not. He shows him a medical certificate drawn up by Kobeliev, justifying his absence from work due to an acute stomach ailment. He tells him that, because they are friends, the doctor doesn't charge him anything, and then whispers in his ear that he resorted to this ruse to visit the wife of a high official who's crazy about him. Pencroff feels his abhorrence for the young man boiling up, now that he's aware of his licentious tendencies. Later the Russian hears about the fight Pencroff had had the day before with one of the workers on the crew, and during the lunch break he seeks him out to ask him what the quarrel was about. Pencroff makes a hand gesture to indicate that he doesn't want to talk about it. You've been in a nasty mood for a couple of days, Zossimov tells him, and asks him if he's angry with him. Pencroff is about to shrug off the burden that has been weighing him down since the night of the dinner party and throw it in his face, noting how conceited Zossimov behaved when he came to his home, strutting around with his wife and her friend, but he saw no grasp of understanding in the Russian's icy gaze that would make him lower himself to apologize, because that would prompt him to understand that the real reason he was upset was jealousy, so he denies being angry with him and tells him, in order to justify his foul mood, that he doesn't like what he and the others are doing down there. The other asks him what he means. We're digging a grave for those who are planning to run away, Pencroff replies. Zossimov gives him an admonishing look to lower his voice, seeing that the other crew members have turned toward them, then asks him if he is on the side of those who decide to escape to West Berlin, making a mockery of the Wall. Pencroff replies that he doesn't like to work on a project where human beings will meet their death. Zossimov exclaims: We're in a war and in war you have to kill.

Pencroff replies: I'm not at war against some poor devils who decide to risk their lives to escape from their own country, and I don't want my children to feel ashamed tomorrow because their father was one of those who dug these death tunnels with his pickaxe. Zossimov lowers his eyes, and Pencroff interprets his gesture as an expression of some unspoken mockery, the meaning of which he intuits: he is too old to have children. Has Sabine told him that he doesn't want to have them? Isn't that proof enough that they've been seeing each other in secret? Zossimov objects, saying that, on the contrary, his children will see him as a hero. Pencroff exclaims: Hero for helping set this perverse trap? The members of the crew have again turned to look at them, but Pencroff no longer cares if they hear him and shouts that the maze is a machine for killing innocent people. Attracted by his shouts, two watchmen come and ask the foreman what's going on. The chief, a man about to retire, replies that they're only joking. The watchmen leave, but not before giving them all an unfriendly look, and the crew return to their work, turning their backs on Pencroff, including Zossimov, who avoids saying goodbye to him as they leave the tunnels.

At the house, seeing his downcast face, Sabine asks him what's bothering him. Pencroff answers that he has a headache, and, using that excuse, he goes to bed right after dinner. He doesn't intend to tell his wife that he's had a fight with Zossimov. When she asks him why, what's he going to tell her, that he hates him because she ogled him when he came to dinner? Nor does he intend to tell her what he said out loud and in front of everyone about the labyrinth, knowing the dire consequences it could have for them.

What could he say to her to justify his outburst? That it disgusts him to participate in the construction of a project where a few desperate people are going to die a slow and atrocious death, when he knows that he uttered those words only because he was jealous? And yet, he feels that what he said isn't entirely false, that those words surfaced as if they'd been held back for a long time, and that if he hadn't uttered them before, not even in front of his wife, it was for fear of being denounced by the neighbors; you never know if they have their ears to the wall or not, ready to denounce you for anything you say against the regime. He remembers Zossimov's words: "We are in a war and in war you have to kill." He rebelled against that lapidary slogan entirely. He didn't feel as if he was at war with anyone, least of all with his compatriots, both on this side of the Wall and on the other. He himself would flee if he had the courage to do so, and so would Sabine, eager as she is to know how people live in other countries. Didn't she ask Zossimov how the women in Moscow dressed, whether they wore makeup or not, and what dances were fashionable in the Russian capital? Then, remembering how excited his wife was when she asked those questions, he feels that perhaps he misjudged her; that maybe he misinterpreted her behavior with Zossimov. She wasn't enraptured with the young Russian, but with the novelty of his presence in the modest apartment where they live. It was the first time since they'd been married that they invited someone to dinner, and she glimpsed through the face of this handsome young man a life that had been denied to them all. Zossimov, quite simply, brought to her apartment the grandiose news that beauty is a real thing; his green eyes represented a dimension of existence that refused to give way under the gray precepts and protocols of Soviet life. How could Sabine and Karla, who spent ten hours a day stuck to machines that pressed out plastic bottles and caps like sausages, not be captivated by the Russian? Yes, Pencroff thinks, his words of indignation, spoken in front of Zossimov, even though they were said out of jealousy, reflected a profound aspect of who he was;

they were prompted by the gloomy existence of this labyrinth that was being forged beneath the city's streets and that, if allowed to reach its completion, would turn them all into living ghosts, if they weren't ghosts already. He takes the card Zossimov has given him out of his pocket and decides that the next day he will go to the Russian embassy to talk to Kobeliev, to ask him to issue a medical certificate exempting him from working underground, whatever it takes. He won't say anything to Sabine, because she won't be happy to see him go back to being a simple bricklayer on a construction site, climbing on scaffolding and earning less than half of what he earns now.

The next day, for the first time since he has been working in the tunnels, he calls his crew chief on the phone to report that he's calling in sick. He complains about a pounding headache, nausea, and body tremors. He waits for Sabine to leave for work before dressing as formally as he can, exhuming a coat and tie he hasn't worn in years, and heads for the Russian embassy, where he asks to speak to Dr. Kobeliev. The receptionist asks him for a reference, and he gives Ivan Zossimov's name. The doctor doesn't keep him waiting and takes him into a small office. He's a short, fat man with sunken eyes in a very large head that looks vaguely like an insect's and never stops moving. Pencroff states his case tersely: working underground is making him claustrophobic, and he knows it isn't a reason for him to be discharged, but he has reached the point where he feels as if he's going insane. Kobeliev, after a cursory examination, suggests that he will write on the certificate that he suffers from acute lumbago, which prevents him from bending down to sink his pick into the ground, and that should be enough to get him out of the tunnels. Pencroff asks him the price, and the other utters a figure that sounds exorbitant to the bricklayer. He tells him that he doesn't know if he'll be able to raise that amount. Do your best and come to see me in eight days, Kobeliev replies, and, still shaking his big head, he gives him a voucher for having missed work.

When Pencroff leaves the embassy, his spirits couldn't be any lower.

With hard work he will be able to raise half of the sum required by the doctor, taking most of it from his and Sabine's savings and borrowing the rest from his father.

It's Friday. He spends the day doing the math and rehearsing the phrases he will use to get his father to lend him the money. On Saturday a demonstration against the GDR government, which has been in the works for weeks, finally breaks out. The younger people, who are familiar with crowds only at the annual military parade on Alexanderplatz, are amazed to see so many people on the streets. Pencroff and Sabine join the crowd, taking care not to give the slightest impression of supporting the protests, and observe everything from a safe distance. On Sunday he receives a call from the crew leader, who informs him that work will be suspended the following day. The existence of the tunnels is an open secret, and the authorities have seen fit to halt work underground until the climate of citizen insurgency dissipates. When he hangs up, Pencroff isn't sure if that was the real reason for the call. Maybe he's been fired for what he said in the tunnels, and tomorrow they'll announce his dismissal. He thinks for a moment about calling Zossimov, who always knows everything, but his pride prevents him from doing so. The afternoon of the next day, he gets another call from the crew leader, who tells him not to show up on Tuesday either. The same thing happens on Tuesday and Wednesday, and Pencroff feels as if he's going crazy. He's afraid that some Stasi officers are going to show up at any moment to arrest him, in which case he will have paid for Kobeliev's medical certificate in vain. He doesn't know what to do and can't get a wink of sleep at night. He finally decides to go through with it and get the certificate and feels inspired to talk to his father, who agrees to lend him the sum he needs. On Thursday morning he goes to pick up the money, and when he returns, he receives another call, this time from Kobeliev. The doctor sounds nervous; he asks Pencroff how much he has managed to put together; Pencroff tells him the sum, which is barely half of what the doctor asked for; the other tells him that it's enough and to bring the money to the embassy the following day. When he hangs up, Pencroff has the feeling that if he had said a smaller amount, Kobeliev would have accepted. The clamor and movement of crowds of people on the street has been increasing. Back from work, Sabine tells him that everyone is in an uproar at the factory. The bosses are continuously moving from one part of the factory to another, as if waiting for a visit from someone important. Rumor has it that

Gorbachev himself is due to come to Berlin that night and a big welcome is being prepared for him in the streets; but according to others the movement in the streets isn't a welcome party at all but rather a massive protest against the Russian leader. Pencroff, who has put the money in an envelope that he will give to Kobeliev the next day, feels like the most miserable person in the world. His life's savings is there, not counting the debt he has just incurred with his father. If he were at least sure that his hatred for the tunnels was genuine, the expense would be justified, but the only thing he's sure of is his jealousy. His jealousy has dragged him down to this point. He wants to get out of the tunnels to be free of Zossimov and Sabine's inexplicable obsession with the labyrinth, which, his instincts tell him, will push her sooner or later into the arms of the young Russian. She's still young and curious, unlike him, whose life has become routine and who is too old to have children. He had that distinct feeling the night he'd invited Zossimov over for dinner. He didn't lift a finger to stake his place in the dinner conversation, experiencing an almost morbid pleasure in seeing how he was ignored. Inwardly, he curses the walled, inescapable society in which he lives. In it, if you suffer some humiliation, there's no way to erase it; it lingers forever, more and more visible to everyone. Suddenly he feels a sharp tightness in his chest and has to sit down. If I could only have a heart attack, he thinks. Maybe then Sabine would forget about Zossimov. He takes a deep breath. His wife has just opened the window, attracted by the noise coming up from the streets.

Then he decides to tell her everything. He will tell her about his jealousy and his argument with Zossimov, about his fear of being fired from his job and his dealings with Kobeliev; and he'll also ask her if she wants to have a child. He stands up and reaches for her standing at the window. He sees that there are masses of other people leaning out their windows like they are. I have to talk to you, he tells her, but Sabine is intent on something the neighbor downstairs is saying and pays no attention to him. Now she's talking to the upstairs neighbor. Suddenly there's shouting in the distance. Everyone's asking what's going on. Two minutes later, at exactly twenty past nine, an extraordinary murmur spreads from window to window. The radio has announced that the Wall has just come down.

THE RAVINE

The father had consulted innumerable catalogs before deciding on this tent. Two days after he bought it, on a Friday afternoon, he wanted to make sure that he would be able to set it up according to the instruction manual, and he thought he would do it on the tree-lined sidewalk that divided the street where they lived. But his wife refused to let him, because she was afraid that the neighborhood, seeing that they were going to spend their summer vacation in an RV park, would conclude that they didn't have the money to afford a fifteen-day stay in a hotel by the sea. So, the family got into the car and the father headed for the outskirts of the city, looking for a vacant lot or a piece of open ground where they could pitch their tent away from the critical gaze of their neighbors.

When they reached the first sorghum fields and a pack of dogs surrounded the car, the father remembered that the farmers used them to guard their property and turned around to go back to the road they had driven on, and that's how they came upon that sandpit at the end of an embankment, a stone's throw from the road, where there was no one except an excavator resting its large articulated arm on the ground. The mother said that it was probably illegal to be there, and her husband, after turning off the engine, replied that it was Friday afternoon and the workers had probably already left. He got out of the car, stood at the edge of the dig site, and looked down. There's a pond, he said, turning toward them. The two sons asked their mother for permission to get out of the car and go see it, but she told them that the sky was extremely cloudy and it wouldn't be long before it rained. She also told her husband, and he replied that there was no rain to be seen, and if it rained it would be okay, because they'd be able to test the tent's waterproofing. She, knowing that it was useless to argue when her husband had an idea in his head, got out of the car with her two children, making sure to bring the umbrella with her. Then he took the two bags containing the tarpaulin and the frame poles out of the trunk, and the four of them descended the ravine's gentlest slope until they reached the edge of the pond, a small round lagoon whose surface was swept by gusts of wind. It was cold and there were small muddy patches here and there across the ground. Some place you brought us, the mother said, and her husband had a hard time finding a piece of land where he could pitch his tent without getting his family's shoes muddy. Germán, the eldest son, helped him remove the poles and spread the tarp on the ground. He was already able to help his father in small tasks and was quite skilled with his hands, unlike Hipólito, the younger one, whose clumsiness with his hands meant that he was considered a perfectly useless member of the family, a stigma that, to be completely honest, was quite convenient for him, because it liberated him from countless obligations. Not all of them, however. The most loathsome was to carry the garbage bags to the basement of the building where they lived, to drop them in the cans that were lined up in a smelly, dimly lit corner. He was terrified, when he went down there, of finding a rat, and as soon as he put the bags down he would rush up the steps to get out of that terrifying cavern.

The mother, seated on one of the fabric folding chairs that were part of the tent's equipment, began to watch her husband and Germán, who had just lined up the metal frame poles on the ground according to their color. Hipólito took advantage of the fact that they had left him behind to approach the edge of the pond, and floated the little plastic boat he had brought, happy to be able to try it out on an actual body of water. He pushed it along, taking care not to let it drift away from the shore, and thoroughly enjoyed the wake that the keel of the little boat formed on the surface. When a gust of wind whipped at the water, he watched in rapture as the plastic toy rocked and rolled, on the verge of sinking. A second gust upset the boat's fragile balance; it capitulated and lay on its side. It was a shipwreck to the letter, and he imitated the sound of the alarm to abandon ship and the cries for help from the crew, while the ship, tossed by the heavy swell, waited for the moment it would go down forever. Absorbed in that drama, he barely heard his mother's voice shouting at him, ordering him to move away from the shore. He stood up, feeling that his feet were soaking wet. His tennis shoes had nearly disappeared under the water. The same swell that had wrecked the boat had covered them up to his ankles. As he stood up, the movement formed a countercurrent that righted the boat and carried it away from the shore. He reached out uselessly to catch it and watched helplessly as it drifted away toward the center of the pond. He felt like crying but held back, knowing that his brother would tease him, call him "baby" or "little woman." It was a new thing between them, something Germán had learned at school. Since he had started second grade, he no longer shared his toys with Hipólito. It was as if the new school year had changed his soul. Hipólito walked to his mother, who removed his tennis shoes and dripping wet socks, rubbed his feet, and ordered her elder son to let his brother use his socks. Germán, totally immersed in the task of setting up the tent, quickly took off his tennis shoes and socks and, after putting his shoes back on, handed the socks to his mother and went back to what he was doing. Hipólito, sitting on his mother's knee, noted with bitterness that his brother hadn't even noticed the boat was lost, floating now in the middle of the pond at the mercy of the currents. His mother hadn't uttered a single word about it either, even though she had seen it drifting away from the shore. As for his father, he could see only the tent at the moment. It was as if the family had all conspired to get rid of that toy so that Hipólito would grow up once and for all, like Germán.

The tent, which up to that moment had been a shapeless canvas slumped across the ground, suddenly rose as Germán and his father pulled the straps from two opposite corners. They did the same with the other two corners, and the tent took shape with all the tension and spaciousness that was contained therein, drawing an ohhh! of wonder from the mother. It was a spacious two-room tent of fiery green and yellow, and now it stood out as the only cheerful note in the desolation of that place. Two men appeared on the opposite side of the ravine from which they had just descended. They wore orange vests and helmets. They came down the sandy slope, and the mother said that they were probably coming to tell them that they couldn't be there. I warned you, she exclaimed, and the father muttered something back, but his words were covered by the roar of an engine behind him. They turned their heads and saw the excavator poised on the edge of the ravine, just above them, its arm topped by a large bucket armored with teeth. She pressed her younger son against her body, in a gesture of protection that didn't fail to frighten Hipólito. He asked his mother what was happening, but she didn't answer him. The two men with helmets had reached the water's edge and were now walking toward them. The father, who was squatting down, pulling one of the tent straps taut, stood up. When the two men reached him, they waved to him by extending their hands and one of them motioned in the direction of the excavator, the engine of which had turned off at that very moment. The driver, a mature, red-haired man, emerged from the cab of the machine, shouted something in the direction of the roadway, and received more shouts in response. In less than a minute, other men in helmets and orange vests appeared. They were carrying wooden planks that they then placed at the base of the excavator, forming a path along the slope where the machine would have to go down. While they were arranging the planks, the red-haired man took out a pack of cigarettes, lit one, and stared at the mother. She returned his gaze, then looked away and noticed the first drops of rain on the surface of the pond. I told your father, she muttered, and opened the umbrella, from which she had not been separated for a moment. She had Hipólito on her knees and couldn't put him down to walk over the muddy ground without his shoes; nor could she carry him to the tent. She called out to her husband, who was showing the tent to the two men and didn't even turn his head. She had no choice but to shout at him, and all of them turned to look at her. Hipólito got his shoes wet and we have to carry him, she exclaimed. I'm coming! her husband said, and continued talking to the two men, one of whom was explaining something to him regarding the pond. In the meantime, two of the guys carrying the planks had approached the mother and had placed some planks on the ground in a row leading up to the tent. They explained that this way her son could walk on them without getting dirty. She thanked them for their kindness and, taking her younger son by the hand, while holding the umbrella with the other, guided him along the wooden path, seconds before the rain began to fall. Her husband was inviting the two men to go inside the tent to cover themselves, and they, after some hesitation, accepted. They greeted Hipólito and his mother with a nod, and the older one, who must have been the boss, removed his helmet out of respect. The father told him to call the guys inside, and when the man hesitated again, he himself went out and shouted for them to come in and take cover. The others didn't hesitate; they left the planks on the ground and came running, but then they hesitated, wondering whether or not to enter the tent, because their boots were caked with mud and they didn't want to get it dirty. The father told them that they wouldn't get it dirty, because in that part of the tent the floor was dirt, and, besides, they'd only set it up to try it out. There were six of them, and when they entered, there were twelve people in the small dining room, all standing and crammed together as if they were in a subway car. The mother then decided to open the bedroom area to better distribute all those people. You can come in here, she said to the young men as she unzipped the divider to show them that attractive extra space, which made them all exclaim in amazement. She asked them to remove their boots because the floor was made of cloth, and they did so obediently, and after taking off their boots and helmets, between laughter and pushing and shoving, they eased into that large inner container, sitting down on the floor with childish glee. As they removed their helmets, she expected to see the red-haired man among them, and, as he wasn't there, she imagined he had stayed in the cab of the excavator to protect himself from the downpour. Somehow, her younger son ended up inside the bedroom, where one of the young men picked him up with both arms and, holding him up, passed him to the guy next to him, who passed him to the guy next to him, in a floating ride that made him laugh out loud. Another one of the younger men picked up Germán, who was watching his brother's progress with rapt attention, and lifted him aloft in the same way. The two boys floated in the space of the bedroom and the guys brought them close to each other, simulating a collision that they accompanied with drawn out exclamations.

When the game subsided, the one who seemed to be the boss of them all asked the guys where Ramón was, and one of them answered that when the rain had started he had preferred to stay with his girlfriend. The others laughed, and the one who looked like the boss felt obliged to explain to his hosts that the girlfriend was the excavator. Then he asked Germán and Hipólito if the little boat floating in the pond was theirs. Hipólito replied that it was his and that the current had pulled it away from the shore while he was playing with it. As soon as the rain is over, let's go and get it, the man said. The father asked how deep the pond was, and his question sparked a heated controversy in the bedroom. Some thought it was simply a puddle, a result of the rains that had fallen over the past few days, but others argued that it was a perennial pond, five to six meters deep, so it wouldn't be so easy to rescue the little boat. In the middle of that discussion, the children's mother told her husband that she was going to the car to get some cigarettes. What cigarettes, he asked. She answered that she had recently discovered an old pack of cigarettes in the glove compartment and had a strong desire to smoke one. Didn't you quit, he asked, and she said nothing, picked up the umbrella, and left the tent.

The rain pattering against the umbrella was so intense that she almost turned back, but looked up at the excavator and walked in that direction, up the plank path that the guys had made on the sand slope for the machine to go down to the bottom of the ravine. When she reached the edge, she approached the excavator and, cupping her hands over her mouth, shouted: Ramón! When there was no answer, she shouted again. The man, who was asleep, straightened up in his seat, looked at her, opened the small sliding glass, and asked her what she wanted. She asked him if he had a cigarette. The man seemed not to understand the question, then reacted and answered yes. The mother asked him if he would give her permission to smoke it inside; he nodded and opened the door. He extended his hand to help her climb in, and because of the momentum that propelled her into the cramped cabin, they practically embraced; they looked into each other's eyes and she smiled nervously.

"This is so small," she said. "You're Ramón, aren't you?" The other answered yes.

"I quit smoking a month ago and I'm dying for a cigarette. I saw you smoking a while ago and that's why I came to see you."

The man told her that she had made the right choice. He addressed her formally and asked her to sit down. There was only one seat in the excavator. She didn't want to:

"You sit, I'm fine standing."

He sat down, took out his pack of cigarettes, offered her one, took out another for himself, and lit them both. Outside it began to hail. They smoked in silence, unable to keep their arms from touching due to the cramped size of the cabin, watching the hail crash against the windshield, and a few minutes later when the hail stopped, she asked him how deep the pond was. The man hesitated before answering, then said no less than three meters.

"Do you see that thing floating in the center? That's Hipólito's little boat, he's my youngest son. It hasn't moved from there and it's his favorite toy. If the pond is really as deep as you say it is, it will be impossible to retrieve it."

The man asked her how old Hipólito was.

"Five."

"I have a son that age," he said.

She asked him what his name was, and he said Manuel. They were silent again, then she asked him how many meters from the shore he estimated the boat to be. Four meters, maybe five, the red-headed man answered. She inhaled deeply, exhaled the smoke with relish, and asked:

"How far does the excavator arm reach?"

The man laughed, rather it was more of a guffaw, and shook his head, looking at her with his dark eyes that she thought were beautiful. She told him. You have beautiful eyes. The other kept shaking his head. What a mother wouldn't do for her child, he exclaimed without stopping laughing, and immediately started the machine's engine. Señora, if you get down, he said, you can tell me if I'm in line with the planks.

"Please, you don't need to be so formal," she said, taking the last puff of her cigarette.

He opened the door so she could get out. The downpour had stopped and the man gave the windshield one last sweep with the wipers before turning them off. He indicated to the woman where to stand and the machine began to move slowly, propelled by the two tracks, until it reached the point where the terrain began to descend. She marked the position of the planks, and when the two crawlers reached the first pair of planks, she took her place in front of the excavator and, walking backward along the slope of the ravine, guided him so that he wouldn't run off the wooden path. In the meantime, the men had come out of the tent, attracted by the noise of the engine. Huddled under the meager canvas roof of the veranda, they gawked as the excavator descended to the edge of the pond, entered into it a few meters, and, extending its powerful arm, lowered its tooth-covered scoop into the water like a glove to pluck out the boy's little boat.

THE BALL IN THE WATER

After separating from Guillermina, Brando rented his house to vacationers during the summer, and he tried to live off the money he earned for the rest of the year. The house was located a few hundred meters from the beach and had only one level, which made it ideal for the elderly and couples with small children. He had been renting it for two years and during those periods he would stay in his aunt Romina's house, about a hundred kilometers from his hometown. His aunt Romina was deaf and used a wheelchair, and two nurses took turns caring for her twenty-four hours a day. She and Brando had never liked each other very much, but he knew that his aunt looked forward to his visits, because he was the only relative she had left and their conversation was much more pleasant than what she had with her two caregivers. This year, however, their cohabitation wasn't going to take place, since his aunt Romina left this world at the beginning of the summer due to a stroke and Brando, who already had his suitcase packed, had to find another place to sleep while his house would be occupied by a young couple with two small children. In the end, his friend Rubén, who lived three houses down from his own and was about to leave for a long trip with his wife to Southeast Asia, offered him a small room with a bathroom at the back of his property, next to the toolshed, in exchange for paying the water, electricity, and telephone bills and cutting the grass in the yard from time to time. Even though they had been friends since high school, this treatment embarrassed Brando. The back room didn't even have a kitchen. If he wanted to cook, Brando would have to make do with an old stove in the laundry area. Rubén told him that if it had been up to him he would have gladly given him one of the rooms in the house; however, Elena, his wife, had flat-out refused; she did not want Brando in her house and was even reluctant to allow him to stay in the back room. Brando merely said that Elena wasn't the only person who disliked him after his separation from Guillermina. What he called separation had consisted of his wife running off with Marcelo, a prosperous gastroenterologist who lived in the next town. That little escapade had allowed Brando to keep the house, and, considering his perpetual state of unemployment, the thing could be considered a gift from the gods, an opinion shared by all his acquaintances, who never forgave him for allowing such a warm and radiant woman as Guillermina to be eclipsed from their lives.

The morning they left for their trip, when the cab was at the door, Rubén gave Brando a copy of the house key, in case "something unusual" happened, a phrase that could mean anything from a fire starting to a coral snake slithering its way in or a thief breaking in. When the cab finally drove away, Brando stayed by the fence for a while, and from there he watched the piece of beach that stretched out in front of his house. The young couple with children were due to arrive later that afternoon. He didn't know them, just as he hadn't met the tenants from the previous two years. The real estate agency took care of everything and on both occasions, after the tenants left, the traces they left behind, such as a coffee or wine stain on the living room carpet, a malfunction in the toilet's flushing mechanism, or a faucet that didn't close properly, had made him feel, for several days, like a stranger in his own home.

The back room of Rubén's house, in addition to a bed and a closet, had a bureau, a small table, and two chairs. Brando opened the windows to air it out, took the table out to the patio, and hung a hammock between the roof drainpipe and a branch of the Australian pine tree, which was the only tree on the property. He stowed what meager clothes he'd brought with him in the closet, checked to see if the bathroom was clean, and made sure Rubén had left enough toilet paper. In addition to a check for two months' worth of food, his friend, behind his wife's back, had left him a handful of cash for extra expenses. Brando didn't like the idea of going to the bank to cash the check, because he knew that by now everyone would have heard that Rubén Gamboa had hired Brando Marcial to be his housekeeper, when just two years earlier, walking into a party on the arm of Guillermina Fuentes, Brando was one of the most envied men in town.

The man and woman probably couldn't have been more than thirty-five years old, he thought as he sat and watched them from under the beach umbrella he had found in the toolshed. Since he didn't like to sit on the sand, he'd brought a plastic chair in addition to the umbrella. He'd also brought a book, a detective novel that he didn't intend to read but that would serve to ward away any acquaintance who might want to greet him.

Every now and then he turned to the young family that had gathered under a large green umbrella. He couldn't make out their faces from where he sat, but from the woman's movements he concluded that she was probably attractive; as for the man, lanky and bald, wearing an old-fashioned bathing suit, he looked like a lawyer or a university professor. The boy and father were playing with a ball, while the mother, lying in the sand, was probably helping the girl dig a tunnel or build a castle. He couldn't imagine a more conventional picture for a family on vacation. He got up and started walking along the seashore, and when he reached the point of the beach where they were, he bent down, pretending to pick up some shells, and looked sideways at the woman, who had just gotten up. She had a nice, slender body, though not very harmonious, as if the different parts hadn't been assembled correctly; but that, far from detracting from her attractiveness, amplified it.

The man and the boy had bent down to look at something in the sand. Brando kept walking until he reached the end of the bay, and when he walked back the family was gone.

He started going to the beach every morning, armed with the umbrella and his novel. After a while he would get up and start walking, pretending to pick up shells but never getting close enough to see the faces of his tenants; until, one morning, the boy failed to catch the ball his father threw him, the ball hit the water, and the current carried it away from the shore. Brando, who was sitting in his usual place, saw the boy run into the water and stand helplessly where the waves were breaking; his father caught up with him and stood there beside him. Apparently, neither of them could swim. Brando got up and walked unhurriedly, because he wanted to give the current time to push the ball a little farther out, then he entered the water, dodged the first waves, and swam in the direction of the ball until he reached it. He was an expert swimmer and returned with the ball against his chest, while the boy jumped up and down with happiness to see that the ball had been safely retrieved. When Brando came out of the water, he handed it to him and the little boy ran triumphantly to his mother, who had been watching the scene sitting under the umbrella; then Brando and the father exchanged a few words. The man told him that they lived in the capital, which he had guessed from his accent; then, grateful for what he had done, the father asked him if he wanted to have a beer and Brando accepted his offer.

He began to visit them every morning and he could tell from the first day that the woman didn't like him. He offered to teach little Cristian to swim and the parents accepted, although not without some hesitation. The boy learned to float under the apprehensive gaze of his mother, who observed the class standing on the shore, holding the towel with which, at the end of the class, she wrapped her son and carried him to the shelter of the shade, as if he had just escaped from some great danger.

The dinner invitation came a week later. It would be a simple dinner, Héctor, the father said, and told him not to bother bringing them anything. He, however, showed up with a bottle of wine he found in Rubén's wine cellar. It was the first time he had used the key to enter his friend's house. He chose a bottle with a recent date, assuming that Rubén, since it wasn't a very old wine, wouldn't notice it was missing.

He had been summoned at eight o'clock and when he was shown in and did not see the children, he asked about them. Elsa, the mother, told him that they had been put to bed because they were exhausted after a full day at the beach. The news made him uneasy. He had brought two gifts for them, a teddy bear for Sabina and an easy-to-assemble model of Cristian's favorite Ninja Turtle, bought at the only toy store in town. I hope they like them, he said, placing them on the table. The father let out a flattering exclamation of surprise, while his wife gave an amused smile.

He made the first mistake of the evening when Héctor, who had his hands full preparing the salad dressing, asked him to open the bottle of wine and, before Héctor told him where the bottle opener was, he went straight to the kitchen drawer where he usually kept it. She noticed and turned her head away from him.

Brando looked around the living room as his hosts busied themselves with preparations, and, although he couldn't say that it looked untidy, he felt a sense of unease at the different way they were using the space he had been lord and master of only a few weeks earlier. They had turned the TV a bit and removed the little pots of cactus on the coffee table, and the Van Gogh reproduction above the sofa was tilted, as if it had been hit by a ball and they hadn't taken the trouble to straighten it again.

When Elsa set the table and said that because there were no wineglasses, they'd drink the wine in regular glasses, Brando couldn't help exclaiming: "There must be wineglasses somewhere," and he started to look for them, until he found them in the lower part of the corner cabinet, where they had always been. To justify his discovery, he said that he knew the people of the town like the back of his hand and he was sure that there would have to be wineglasses in a house like this one. The woman gave her husband a look and Brando realized that he had made the second mistake of the night.

During dinner, Elsa took only a few tiny sips from her wineglass, and to him each one seemed like a declaration of war; it was as if with each sip she was reassuring him that she was drinking her wine out of mere politeness, refusing to savor it. Her husband asked a few questions about the town, also out of pure courtesy, for it was evident that the subject didn't interest him in the least and Brando thought they were the kind of people who, when vacationing in a seaside town, cared only about the waves and the sand. One of the questions Héctor asked him was if he knew the owner of that house; he said he did not and explained that before that beach had become so trendy, everyone knew everyone, but now many rented their houses during the summer or even half the year, and the sense of community had been lost.

Elsa went to bed after coffee, adducing a headache, and with her, who clearly disliked him, gone, Brando felt the evening had lost its only appeal. Hector's chatter bored him (he was a naval engineer and was telling him how many containers could fit on a state-of-the-art cargo ship), and when Héctor suggested opening another bottle, Brando said he had to leave because he had to deal with an urgent matter first thing the next day. They said goodbye and he decided to walk home along the beach instead of the causeway.

He let a week pass before inviting them to dinner. He prepared spaghetti with ragu, his only culinary talent, accompanied by a potato salad he bought at the supermarket. His guests arrived on time. Along with a bottle of red wine they brought a large bowl of rice pudding. They praised the house, and, for once, Elsa was pleased with what her eyes were seeing. However, when she asked him if he had cinnamon for the rice pudding, Brando said he couldn't remember and couldn't tell her where the spices were. All she had to do was open the first kitchen cabinet to find them. They were too visible for him to have forgotten where they were, and he justified himself by saying that the cleaning lady was always moving things around.

After dinner she went out to the backyard to smoke a cigarette. The children played in a corner of the living room and called their father to show him something. Brando cleared the table and when Elsa returned after five minutes, she told her husband that she had a headache and ordered the children to pick up their toys, because it was time to leave. Brando walked them to the front gate and as they walked away he saw her talking heatedly to her husband. Brando had a gut feeling and headed for his room in the back. He found the door open. He was sure he had closed it, as he always did to keep the mosquitoes out, and he realized that she must have gone in to nose around. His detective novel, which she knew well because Brando always carried it with him, was on the bedside table. He imagined that the woman had put two and two together. That wasn't his house and he lived in that little room. Her headache had been a pretext for ending the evening early.

The next day, when he approached the family encampment on the beach and Elsa took a few steps forward to tell him that the swimming class would be canceled because Cristian had had a bad night, he knew that they no longer wanted to have anything to do with him. The boy, lying on the sand with his bucket and shovel, avoided looking at him. Héctor, sitting on his beach chair, read a book and had his back turned to him. Only the little girl, too small to follow her parents' instructions, smiled at him as she did every day. Standing in front of that invisible wall erected by the family, he avoided the humiliation of returning the way he had come and walked to the seashore, entered the water, and swam out to sea until he was tired. When he stopped, the beach was a thin line that intermittently disappeared with the movement of the swell. He had never been so far out to sea before and slowly made his way back to the beach, wondering if they were watching him.

Back in his room, he was assaulted by the image of the Van Gogh painting hanging lopsided in his living room and felt that carelessness was an affront. That night the mosquitoes focused all their rage on him and he woke up in a lousy mood; he spent the morning going back and forth from his hammock to the fence, from where he could see them. He thought he could insist that they show him the house to see if they'd damaged it; it was his house after all and he had every right to check every room.

He showed up at eight o'clock, as if he had been invited over for dinner. It was a hot night, a stream of dark clouds was advancing from the horizon, and the wind brought an amplified sound of the swell. When he rang the doorbell he noticed a whisper of movement in the dining room curtains and knew he was being watched. He rang again and heard footsteps. Héctor, without opening the door, asked what he wanted. To have a word, if you don't mind, he said, and tried to make his voice as calm as possible. Let's talk tomorrow, was the reply that came from inside. I'd rather talk now, I won't bother you again, he replied. He heard some murmuring. Husband and wife were arguing in hushed tones. The door finally opened and Héctor, standing in the doorway to block his way, asked him again what all this was about. Behind him, shielding herself with her husband's body, Elsa looked at him with a mixture of supplication and revulsion. From where he stood, he saw that the Van Gogh painting was still tilted, as it had been the week before.

"I can't believe it!" he said.

"What?"

"That you still haven't straightened the painting." He pointed his finger at the painting on the back wall. Héctor turned to look and Brando took advantage of this oversight to enter the house. Elsa let out a scream. Brando walked to the far end of the room, straightened the painting, stepped back a few feet to see if it was straight, and then corrected the tilt with a tap on the frame. "This is my house!" he exclaimed.

"Get him out of here, he's crazy!" Elsa shouted, and Brando saw that she was wielding a kitchen knife.

"Get out!" Héctor shouted, and then repeated in a lower voice, "Get out! We know it's your house."

There was a sound of crying. It was the little girl, who had begun to call for her mother. The three stood listening to the sobs coming from the back room.

"Go see what she needs," Héctor said to his wife.

"I'm not moving from here until he leaves." Elsa nodded her head at Brando.

Brando thought it was a little pitiful the way she was holding the knife and thought it would have been easy enough to take it out of her hand. He looked at them and said:

"Who do you think you are? You think you own the world? All the beaches look the same to you, all the people you don't know look the same to you. This is my house and I want you to respect it!"

"We already know it's your house," Héctor replied.

"How do you know?"

"We talked to the agency."

"Aren't you smart."

"Please, Brando," Elsa begged, "get out of here. We promise we'll take care of your house. You'll find everything the way you left it. We're decent people."

"This is the first time you've called me by my name," he said. "We've known each other for two weeks and this is the first time you've called me by my name."

"I hadn't noticed. That doesn't mean I don't respect you."

"I couldn't tell with that knife in your hands."

Elsa was silent but kept the knife in the same position, ready to use it against him. The girl was still crying.

"Go see what's wrong with her," Héctor said, but Elsa didn't even look at him. She was looking at Brando and Brando was looking at her.

"Please, get out," the woman begged again. "The children are getting really nervous."

Brando had the feeling that this was the first time he and Elsa had ever looked at each other. It was a look that excluded Héctor and he wondered what she had seen in this naval engineer who knew the exact number of containers that would fit on a state-of-the-art cargo ship. The girl had stopped crying and the sound of the waves drifted up to them.

"I taught your son how to swim," he exclaimed, looking at Elsa, as if Héctor didn't exist.

"And we appreciate that," Héctor said. "We'll never forget it. But now, please get out."

Brando continued to look at the woman, without a single glance at her husband, and he knew that she would never forget his face and his name, nor the noise of the waves crashing that night, and, satisfied, he walked toward the door. Héctor stepped aside to let him pass, Brando climbed over the wooden fence, and they watched him head for the beach and closed the door.

The downpour lasted all night. He had to give up the hammock and sleep in the shack. Even with the roar of the rain, he could hear the waves crashing on the shore. As always when it rained at night, he thought of Guillermina, who adored the night rains and said that they were the best sleeping pill there was.

He had a restless night, and when he woke up he was overcome by the image of Elsa wielding the kitchen knife, her face on the verge of tears, and he had no doubt that she had burst out crying as soon as he'd left. He was suddenly seized with fear that they would decide to leave, demanding the agency return their money or a portion of it. He left the room and walked to the fence. They were usually on the beach at that hour and his heart skipped when he didn't see anyone. Half an hour later he took the key to Rubén's house and went inside to call the rental company. A woman answered and Brando told her that he was calling to let them know that the contact phone number he had provided, which was his aunt's, was no longer in use and to please write down another one. He gave Rubén's number, with the clarification that they could only reach him there from seven to eight at night. The woman thanked him for the information and Brando asked her if there was any news about the people who rented his house. What kind of news? the woman asked. I don't know, anything, he answered. Give me a moment, and it took her a little while to pick up the receiver again and inform him that there was no news. Brando thanked her, hung up, locked the house door, and walked to the fence. The beach was still empty. He returned to his room, took out the hammock, which he hung under the Australian pine tree, and picked up the detective novel. It was hot and the patio was already dry after the night's downpour. He stretched out in the hammock, opened the book, read the first page, and fell asleep.

He went to the fence several times throughout the afternoon to look. No one was there. A little before seven o'clock he went into Rubén's house in case there was a possible call from the agency. He sat in the dining room from seven o'clock until a quarter past eight. As he was leaving the phone rang. He felt his stomach drop and picked up the phone. It was a woman's voice, asking for Elena. Elena isn't here, he answered. The woman said she was

Elena's aunt. Rubén isn't there either? she asked. No, they went on a trip and will be back at the end of the summer, Brando said. Of course, I forgot, the woman exclaimed, remained silent for a few seconds and said she would call back, thanked him and hung up. Brando did the same and realized that his hands were shaking.

The next day dawned cloudy and the wind picked up, and as the heat had dropped he was motivated to cut the grass in the yard and prune the Australian pine, tasks that he had been putting off because of the heat. Every now and then he went to the fence to see if they were there. They didn't show up all day and he was seriously thinking about the possibility that that they had left. At seven o'clock that evening he went back to sit in the dining room of Rubén's house, in case the agency called him. While he waited he poured himself half a glass of whiskey. He would have preferred gin, but there was only a third of its contents and he thought Rubén might notice a drop in the level of liquid in the bottle. The agency didn't call and at eight o'clock he locked up and went back to his room.

He had a hell of a night: he'd forgotten to close the window and the mosquitoes went on their rampage until dawn. He managed to sleep for a while, and after he woke up and walked to the fence (it had become an almost mechanical movement), his heart stopped for a moment when he recognized the green umbrella on the beach. So they were back, or rather, they hadn't left. He went to town to pay Rubén's electricity, water, and gas bills, bought some food, and returned at noon. In the afternoon he made another attempt at the detective novel and managed to read the entire first chapter. For the first time he admitted that he had missed them. The swimming lessons he gave Cristian, little Sabina's smiles, Elsa's cubist body, and even Héctor's lectures on cargo ships had been the best thing that had happened to him since Guillermina had run off with her stupid gastroenterologist. He remembered how Elsa, knife in hand, had called out his name. Please, Brando, she'd said. Please, Brando, he muttered to himself, trying to reproduce her voice. He couldn't and felt a little embarrassed.

That night, about to fall asleep, he imagined the boy's ball ending up in the water again and the current pushing it away from the shore; Cristian screamed as his father watched helplessly while the ball drifted out to sea; he, who was sitting under his umbrella, walked slowly toward the water and, swimming diagonally, reached the ball, returned with it to the beach, and handed it to the boy, who thanked him and ran triumphantly to his mother, who, standing, had been watching everything; the father, then, taking a few steps toward him, extended his hand and thanked him. This point of the story didn't satisfy him and he modified it. Sometimes he responded to that handshake; sometimes he didn't. Then he found the solution: the father, instead of shaking his hand, would give a slight nod of his head as a sign of thanks; he would respond in the same way, and turn around and go back to his spot on the beach.

A week had passed since they had stopped speaking to each other. That night, at eight o'clock, the phone rang.

He ran to the bureau in his little room to search for the keys, then opened the door to Rubén's house, and when he reached the machine, the phone stopped ringing. He sat down to wait and, taking advantage of the situation, poured himself a glass of whiskey. The phone rang again, he picked it up, and a woman's voice asked for Mr. Brando. Speaking, he said. I'm Señora Olga, Elena's aunt, do you remember me, the voice asked. Brando recognized the woman he had spoken to a few days earlier. Yes, I remember, he said. I spoke to my niece yesterday, who offered me her house until the end of the summer, as you know, the woman said. Brando didn't answer right away, then mumbled: I wasn't aware of that, no. I thought you had been told, you're the caretaker, aren't you? Brando didn't know what to say. The other asked again, raising her voice: You are the caretaker, Mr. Brando, aren't you? Brando answered: I am, yes. The woman breathed a sigh of relief and added: My two sisters and I will be arriving tomorrow afternoon. I have a list of things I desperately need you to buy, Mr. Brando. Do you have something to write with?

THE MONT BLANC TUNNEL

The French and Italian workers digging the tunnel that will pass through Mont Blanc, linking France with Italy, are about to meet. Only a meter and a half of rock remains to be bored through to complete the titanic excavation that began five years, four months, and sixteen days earlier. The meeting is scheduled for 2:21 p.m., when the last piece of feldspathic rock that obstructs the passage between the two countries will fall under the impact of the jackhammers. The foremen for both teams will be in charge of the last bit of hammering and boring and shake hands through the opening in the rock, a handshake that will be televised across Europe. The opening will then be widened enough to allow the French team to move to the Italian side, where there will be a toast with speeches in both languages, all of this taking place under the 4,810 meters of granite that represents the height of the highest peak in the Alps. It is worth noting that the two teams of workers already know each other, because they met at the beginning of the project, three days before a jackhammer made the first perforation on the French side. There were also toasts and speeches on that occasion. And this brings us to the matter that interests us most. On that day, the Italian worker Gianluca Rondolotti and the French worker Julien Lambert began a sturdy friendship (rarely has that adjective been applied with more relevance) that would turn into a successful business relationship when Rondolotti decided to invest the sum of a small inheritance in a business that sold and installed double-glazed windows, a business that Lambert would be in charge of starting up in Nantes, his hometown. The two met twice in Nantes to work out the details, and a month later Lambert opened a shop three blocks from his home. As he worked in the Mont Blanc tunnel, his sister Luiselle, who turned out to be a keen businesswoman with a good nose for market practice, took charge of the shop. Gianluca's sister, Tiziana Rondolotti, who had recently graduated with a degree in foreign languages and specialized in French, dealt with all client correspondence and communications. Soon she and Luiselle took over the reins of the business, in which Gianluca and Julien, consumed by their work in the tunnel, intervened only when important decisions had to be made. After a difficult start, the business prospered rapidly. But let's get to the point. On the day of the tunnel's completion, when the teams of workers from both sides gathered to toast, Gianluca Rondolotti gave Julien Lambert, on behalf of his sister Tiziana and for Julien to pass on to Luiselle, a shoebox adorned with a bow. The box contained a turtle, a birthday present from Tiziana to Luiselle, who adored these animals. Tiziana, aware of the fact that sending the turtle by post would have been extremely complicated and expensive, and taking into account that the next day Gianluca would meet Julien in the Mont Blanc tunnel, thought that the most expeditious way to get her gift to Luiselle would be to give the box to her brother. The box did not go unobserved: Lambert and Rondolotti were asked what it contained, as well as the reason for its delivery through the tunnel, and when Rondolotti opened it and the turtle popped its head out, all the workers wanted to have their picture taken with it. It wouldn't have gone any further, except that the next day someone remarked in front of the television cameras that the turtle was the first living creature to cross through the recently completed tunnel. The governments of both countries thought it was a good omen that the first user to benefit from that magnificent undertaking was an animal traditionally associated with wisdom and prudence, as they feared that many people would not want to use the tunnel for fear of a collapse, a fire, or any other incident that could prove disastrous in the depths of the mountain. Thus, Luiselle Lambert's tortoise became the symbol of the Mont Blanc tunnel and the most photographed tortoise in the world practically overnight, and still today, when crossing the tunnel, a beautiful stone effigy of the creature can be seen at the entrance on both sides, which many motorists misinterpret as an appeal to drive slowly.

THE SHADOW OF THE MAMMOTH

It was the only part of the cave smooth enough to paint on. Since the light from the outside barely illuminated it, the man who was drawing a hunting scene had to make a fire so he could see the rock wall. He used the charcoal pieces he kept in a clay pot to outline each figure: men with bows and spears on one side, animals on the other (bison and deer). His lines were uncertain; he evaluated them by moving away from the wall and then he redrew them again and again. What he redrew the most were the animals. He wanted to draw them escaping from men, but he couldn't find a way to convey the terror that made them want to run away. He closed his eyes to re-create a mental image of the beasts galloping, trying to evoke the position of each leg, but when it was time to transfer that position to the drawing something got lost or distorted in his head.

The man who lived on the seventh floor had been a member of the fitness center across the street from his apartment for a few months. He ran for half an hour on the outdoor track three nights a week. "Ran" is one way of saying it. Forty-some years old, he jogged, but it was a sustained jog, which after seven laps left him exhausted. From the height of his apartment he had a full view of the all-weather track and liked to watch the runners from his living room window. He recognized many of them by the way they ran. It surprised him how each had a unique style, precise as a fingerprint, that made them unmistakable from a distance.

He translated books and technical articles and had few friends, whom he rarely saw. Mondays, Wednesdays, and Fridays, just as it was starting to get dark, he would get ready to go to the track. He left his apartment in his sweatpants and sweatshirt and would leave the living room light on. As he ran around the track, he would look up at that one lit window, as if it were a beacon in the night. It had cost him a great deal of sacrifice to buy that seventh-floor apartment, but now that it was his he felt that his existence had meaning, and he was proud to own it when he was still in the prime of his life. He'd worked extremely hard to get it, giving up, among other things, starting a family. He didn't regret it much, but he couldn't help thinking that if he had married and had one or two children, he would now be more adventurous, more dynamic.

He had been born into a different tribe from the one he lived in now and had lived for a time in a third tribe, which meant he could speak three different languages; although they were quite similar, their difference was like an insurmountable wall when it came to settling tribal disputes. Therefore, whenever the tribes had to reach an agreement because of some problem between them, he served as a translator. "Translator" is an understatement, because it took him a long time to reproduce in one language what had been said in another. Each sentence made him sweat profusely, and it is likely that if he had not sweated, no one would have believed him, because they didn't fully grasp what he was doing or how he did it. Even he, if he had to explain it, wouldn't have found the right words. He'd resigned himself to the fact that his people didn't fully trust him and forced him to live in a hut far from everyone else, almost on the edge of the tribe's territory, even though it was because of him they could communicate with neighboring tribes. He didn't join the hunts with the other men, nor did he help the women with their tasks, and every third day some old women would leave him some pieces of meat, tubers, and fruit at the entrance to his hut. He had no wife or children, and it wasn't clear whether the women didn't want to be with him or it was he who didn't feel inclined to have a companion.

The last time he'd been called upon for his skills in enlightening each tribe on the words spoken by opposing tribes had been before the rains. The problem once again had to do with the cave, which the three tribes used as a shelter during their winter hunts. The negotiation dragged on amid misunderstandings that at one point almost led to open conflict. In the end, the decision was made to prohibit any hunter from entering the cave and instead to use it as a place for the burial of the dead. In reality, it being a place of difficult access, no one intended to bury their dead there, and it was satisfaction enough for each group to know that the others wouldn't use it for their hunting parties. They agreed that he, the translator, should be in charge of the place, although it wasn't made clear how. He was supposed to keep an eye on it, but it wasn't said how, or how often. Afterward he had a dream in which he and the other men were chasing a wounded bison. They were running after the big animal, certain they would be able to bring it down, and this enraged them with joy. When he woke up, he decided that he would write that dream on the cave wall. He had learned to trace on stone with pieces of charcoal while living in the third tribe. He lived there for a year and when he was released he returned to his tribe of origin, which no longer accepted him because he used so many words of the tribe that had captured him. Thus he wandered alone for some time, until he was adopted by his present tribe, and since he had lived there he hadn't once picked up a piece of charcoal to draw a figure of man or animal. Now the dream of the bison hunt had reminded him of that skill. On his next visit to the cave he looked for a surface smooth enough to draw on and found it far from the entrance, where the daylight was so weak that a fire had to be lit to illuminate the wall.

The runners who used the track were the people with whom the man who lived on the seventh floor interacted most assiduously. He would greet several and several of them would greet him, but no one knew his name and he knew none of theirs. It was a fraternity based on sweat. However, there were also conflicts. The most frequent was when someone who didn't run very fast would occupy the innermost lane of the all-weather track, traditionally intended for the faster runners. The latter were forced to overtake the slower runner, thus breaking the rhythm of their pace, and there's nothing more irritating to a high-performance athlete than breaking the rhythm of their stride. Fights erupted, some of which had come close to blows. So he confined himself to the fourth lane, where he was in no one's way.

He was doing some push-ups after finishing his usual seven laps when a gray-haired man came up to him and introduced himself. The man said that he was he was organizing a group of runners in lane number four to jog together on Mondays, Wednesdays, and Fridays from seven to eight in the evening. The idea was to run as a group because many were bored with running alone, and doing it as a group would also help them maintain a steady running pace. Mature people, he specified, which translated into athletic terms meant a moderate jog. He didn't need to think about it to agree, and in a way he had been hoping for this moment since he had joined the club. He was tired, after two months, of not knowing anyone; he missed saying the names of others and hearing his own name in the mouths of others. He thanked the gray-haired man for his invitation and told him he would try a few laps to see if he could keep up with the pace of the others and, if he couldn't, he would keep running on his own. They shook each other's hand warmly and said goodbye, and on Monday he showed up on time for the appointment. The gray-haired man was doing warm-up exercises in the area at the edge of the Olympic track, and, as soon as he saw him, he came over to apologize. He told him that the other people in the group had a last-minute hitch and weren't going to make it. He asked how many there were and the man gave him a vague answer, which led him to suspect he was lying to him. The other man called someone's name and a teenager who was sitting on the grass outside the track got up and, hesitating, walked toward them. He's my son, the man said, and, turning to the boy, he directed his steps by saying, "To your right, Manuel." He realized that the son was blind and had to take a step to his left so that his hand and the boy's could meet. We run together, the father explained, and then tied his wrist to his son's wrist with an elastic band. Ready, he exclaimed, and he, who had never seen a blind man run on the track, tried to hide his surprise. They entered the track and headed for the fourth lane. The father asked him to go ahead and he started slowly, as was his custom; then, little by little, as he warmed up, he increased his pace. After a lap and a half the father and son fell behind. He could hear the breathing of both and knew that the one who wasn't able to keep up was the old man. So he stopped and when the others caught up, he asked the father if he wanted to give him the elastic band. The old man didn't make him say it twice; he took it off and looped it around his wrist. When he and the son began to run, bound together like that, the old man crossed the track to lie down on the grass, exhausted; that's when he understood that the whole story about the mature running team had been a fabrication to win over his friendship and palm his blind son off on him.

One morning, after lighting the fire, he found some female footprints in the cave. He noticed that the right heel print was deeper than the left heel, from which he deduced that the woman was carrying a baby. It was unusual for a woman to venture to such a remote place alone, and even more so carrying a small child in her arms. She must have spent the night in the cave to protect herself from animal attacks, and he determined that she'd been expelled from her tribe. He looked for the traces of a fire, but didn't find any. Either the woman didn't know how to light a fire or she hadn't so she wouldn't give herself away. She must have been very young, judging by the size of her footprints, which indicated that the feet were still childlike, so the child she was carrying must have been her first. If the two of them were on their own, he thought, their days were numbered. He decided that after spending the night in the cave, the woman must have left because the drawings on the wall had warned her that the place had an owner. He had drawn three men armed with bows, several bison, and two deer; he intended to add several more men, some with spears, but when he set out to draw them, what he saw was no hunter at all but a woman with a child in her arms, and he was astonished to see that such a well-drawn figure had come out of his hand.

Two days later he came across the same footprints. The woman had spent the night in the cave again, but this time she had lit a fire and that reassured him. Apparently, she was not entirely incapable of getting by. Thinking that perhaps she might return to the cave, he had brought a piece of meat with him and left it by the fire stones, wrapped in a piece of fur. Then it occurred to him to press his footprints next to the young woman's tracks. If she wasn't a fool and observant enough to notice them, she would understand that it was a sign of friendship. He knew she had looked at his drawing, because her footprints were next to the wall, and he imagined her sitting on the ground, looking at the bison and deer as she nursed the little one; maybe she wondered if she was that figure of the woman carrying a child. He also found remains of food: acorn shells, seeds, and nuts. There was no indication that she had eaten meat. So she was truly alone, with no one to hunt for her, which was as bad as not knowing how to start a fire, for with only acorns and tubers she wasn't going to make it through the winter.

He had brought some yellow pigment with him, which he intended to use to fill in the figures of the bison, but before he did that he had to correct some of the marks he had made with the charcoal. Now that he knew that the woman was looking at his drawings, he discovered some defects he hadn't seen before. What had come out best was the woman carrying her young child, and he thought that maybe that drawing had encouraged the young mother to return to the cave. He thought that the drawings might have turned out so well because he wanted her to return.

The first thing he did the next day was to check if the chunk of meat was still where he had left it, and he was deeply relieved to see that it was gone. The piece of fur had been folded up again, which he interpreted as a gesture of thanks. So she had come for the third time, which meant she would keep coming back for warmth and food, and the revelation that she was now dependent on him disturbed him. It was a new feeling, and he immediately feared for her, because he was all too familiar with the sudden mood swings of these men and knew that, when the winter became more severe, they would forget their agreements and once again use the cave for their hunting trips. Unless he managed to scare them off with the figures he painted on the wall. But with deer and bison the size of the palm of his hand, he wasn't going to scare anyone. He needed something big, and he thought of a mammoth, a mammoth with a huge head and formidable tusks that would fill the cave wall from floor to ceiling, as if a mammoth had forgotten its shadow on the wall when it emerged from the cave. If he succeeded in painting the shadow of a mammoth, the men would think the animal might come back for it at any moment and that would scare them away.

It took him one lap around the track before he could match the blind kid's rhythm, but from then on their breathing came together in puffs that merged them in a way he would never have believed possible. He was overcome by an animal-like feeling of plenitude that would linger in his bones for several hours, leaving him euphoric but also profoundly sad, as he realized how little joy he had known in his life. It was on the third lap, as they rounded the curve of the track facing north, that he noticed the bizarre figure that, due to the cross play of the overhead lights, cast the shadow of his body with that of the boy's body, joined at the wrists: an amazing animal with two large fangs. On the next lap, when the figure was repeated identically, he was overcome by the helplessness of not being able to show it to the other, who was running unaware of the small miracle that the all-weather track gave them at that point. The apparition returned during the next three laps, first the four legs and a second later, as if in a flash, the large head armed with two magnificent tusks, created by their two arms tied together. He thought of a mammoth. When at last they stopped, as they huffed and wheezed to catch their breath, he looked for a way to communicate his discovery to the boy, but he was afraid of appearing ridiculous and decided that he wouldn't tell him about it until they knew each other a little better. Two nights later, however, the father was the only one who showed up at the track. He told him that his son hadn't come because he was a little under the weather. He tried to hide his disappointment, because he still felt the bodily intoxication that came from running attached to the young man's arm, their sweat and breath mixing and then, as if it were some consequence of that melding, the magic of that apparition halfway around the curve facing north, the prehistoric mammoth produced by their shadows joined at the wrists, surfacing for a few seconds on the all-weather track with the precision of a cave painting. He concealed his frustration so badly that when he began to run with the old man, he ahead and the other following him, he hardly noticed that he was increasing the distance that separated them, overwhelmed as he was by the sadness of exercising all alone around a circle, in a middle lane for average runners, which seemed like a reflection of his own life, also average and lacking in emotions.

He was going to need a very long ladder to reach the high cave ceiling, and a ladder of that size could be erected only with someone's help. He thought of Oruuz, who was not only strong but also blind. He did not, in effect, want anyone to see his figures on the wall. He had hoped that the outline of the mammoth, once finished, would look like a real shadow and not a drawing. He went to talk to Anat, the tribal chief and Oruuz's brother, and told him that he needed his brother's help for three days to build a ladder to reach the highest part of the cave, where he planned to dig a niche in the rock to hold the skulls of the dead, because at that distance from the ground the wolves would be unable to reach them. Anat reluctantly agreed, because he didn't like to part with his burly brother, who was the tribe's strongest beast of burden.

The next day he and Oruuz climbed up to the cave. With fallen branches and other thicker ones that Oruuz cut with his flint knife, they put together the central part of the ladder; the next day they collected leaves from the ayesnis, the plant that grew at the foot of the oaks, from which they pulled the fibers that would be used to tie the branches together, and they spent the third day assembling the rungs. They slept by the fire, and he could hardly sleep a wink, because he thought that the young mother, seeing that the cave was occupied at night, would go away forever. On the fourth day he and Oruuz lifted the ladder. Just as it was almost completely up, the structure tottered and broke in half and crumbled to the ground. They had to put the parts back together with more strands of ayesnis fiber, which took them the rest of the morning and all afternoon. Finally they were able to lift it to its full length and lean it against the wall. He climbed up very slowly, while Oruuz held it from below, and when he reached the ceiling of the cave and looked down to the ground, his legs trembled and he wondered how he was going to paint from that height. Before returning to the village he left a piece of meat wrapped in the strip of fur by the fire circle, and the first thing he did the next morning was unwrap it. The meat was gone. The woman had been careful to refold the cloth to make it clear that this was not the work of an animal, and he was moved by this new gesture of understanding. The tracks of her footprints went along the wall, and the earth beneath the fire circle was warm from the fire she had lit in the night. He had missed her, and despite the danger of climbing to the top of the ladder, he began that very day to paint the shadow of the mammoth that he hoped would protect the young mother and her little one.

He soon realized that to cover the width of the drawing it would be necessary to move the ladder along the wall, and he went back to Oruuz for help. When he and the blind giant arrived at the cave, Oruuz wanted to light a fire for warmth and noticed that the ground where the fire pit was located was warm, a sign that someone had spent the night in the cave and lit a fire there. I left here late last night and forgot to put the fire out, he lied, but Oruuz said that the branches in the bonfire had been thin and with them the fire would have gone out quickly, while the warmth of the ground showed that it had been fed throughout the night. Then it appears that a morning draft came into the cave and fanned the embers, he said, in another attempt to justify the heat given off by the floor around the fire. This explanation didn't convince the blind man either, who repeated that no air current could reach that point of the cave with enough vigor to stoke the embers, and he repeated that a hunter had spent the night there and eaten meat. Then he turned to look at him, as if he had forgotten that he was blind, because, as he had recently lost his sight, he still had many gestures of the people who see. Have you let the river men come in here, he asked, and he protested, raising his voice in indignation at the suspicion, the accusation, that he had betrayed his people. Oruuz didn't show any sign of fear, but merely looked at him from his empty eye sockets, and in that sinister look he saw the entire concentration of distrust that these tribesmen had for him. He knew that that same day, back in the huts, Oruuz would tell his brother that the floor where the fire had been was warm, a sign that people from the river had spent the night in the cave, and his hair stood on end, imagining how Anat would get angry, blame him for the intrusion of the rival tribe. While the blind man lit the fire, he erased the footprints the woman had left everywhere and noticed that the impression her right heel made was now deeper, a sign that the baby had gained weight. Then, while Oruuz slept by the fire, he climbed to the top of the ladder and began to apply a clay paste inside the outline of the large animal, burying with it the figures of deer and bison from his first drawing. From the latter he decided to save only the figure of the mother carrying a child, because he wanted it to coexist with that of the mammoth. Thus, perhaps, if the men found the young woman inside the cave, they wouldn't dare harm her, believing that she was somehow linked to the animal by some indestructible bond.

On Friday night the father once again showed up at the track alone and told him that his son still had a cold. He was hesitant to believe him and thought that maybe the son needed a faster runner, and the father didn't want to tell him so his feelings wouldn't be hurt. He was overcome with despair at the prospect of never seeing the young man again, and when the father asked him where he lived, he merely pointed to the lighted window on the seventh floor. The other raised his eyes, looked at the rectangle of light that was silhouetted against the sky, and said that he was fortunate to have such an excellent view of the track. He didn't miss the opportunity these words offered him, thanked the man for the compliment, and told him that he would have liked to invite him and his son for a late meal one evening the following week, after they ran, to enjoy the view of the track from above. He didn't consider it awkward to include his blind son in the enjoyment of that view, and the father seemed not to notice anyway, nor did he give it any importance, because he replied that he and Manuel would be delighted to see his apartment. Could they do it the following Monday, he asked, anxiously. Certainly, the man said, saying goodbye and shaking his hand.

The only thing left to do was to remove the ladder so that the large drawing could be seen in its entirety, and again he asked Oruuz for help. The blind man didn't have to be asked twice and took a leather bag with him, inside which he kept some of his dead father's bones. He wanted him to place them in the niche he had been carving along the top of the wall. Anat commanded it. He had, in effect, been digging a modest niche in the rock to justify the use of the large ladder. He took the leather bag Oruuz handed him and climbed to the top. The blind man, who was holding the ladder from below, asked him if he had already reached the top; he answered that he had and took the bones out of the bag to place them where the other had ordered him to. Those are dog bones! Oruuz exclaimed, and pushed the ladder with all his strength, which, when it collapsed, carried in its fall its unsuspecting passenger, who crashed face-first to the ground, splitting his head in two.

He was busy all Monday afternoon preparing dinner. He would serve a pork tenderloin, cucumber salad with yogurt, and white wine, with crème brûlée for dessert. Every now and then he would stop watching the tenderloin roast in the oven to go to the living room window and look out onto the track. It was the first time since he'd bought the apartment that he would have guests. When it got dark and the overhead lights came on, he scanned the track again for the old man and his son. They weren't there. He berated himself for not having asked the father for his cell number, and for not having given him his own. He turned the oven off and started to get dressed to go to the track. His heart was pounding, as it always did when he had a bad feeling. He walked down the seven flights of stairs, lest the elevator stop for some reason, crossed the street, and entered the fitness center. When he walked onto the outdoor track, after checking to be sure that the father and son weren't there, he felt a new sense of uneasiness. There was still time, he thought, but he knew they wouldn't come. He did push-ups to warm up and ten minutes later made his way to the fourth lane to begin his workout. As he ran, he kept his eyes on the entrance to the track. He still hadn't given up hope that they might show up at any moment. Coming out of the curve facing north, he took advantage of the track's straightaway to close his eyes. He wanted to experience for a moment what it was like for the blind son to run. He opened them five seconds later and saw that he had crossed into the third lane. He immediately moved back to his own lane, to the fourth lane, where he wasn't in the way of any runner. He wasn't blind, thank God, and didn't need to run tied to anyone's arm.

In the days that followed, from the moment the sports center opened, he would interrupt his work to stand at the living room window, searching for the two silhouettes on the track. Perhaps they had changed their schedule, he thought, and when he went down at night to train, he ran with the illusion that they would appear at any moment.

A year later the number of his laps around the outdoor track had risen from seven to nine, he was still in the fourth lane out of habit, and everyone called him by his name. One night—it was a Wednesday—as he was limbering up on the edge of the track, he saw them. They were in the third lane. They were running at the same pace. He guessed that they were both in their thirties. The blind man was a little shorter than the other and they were bound together at the elbows by an elastic band. He figured that once he gained the trust of the two young men and ran a few laps tied to the one who couldn't see, it wouldn't be hard to convince him to move over to the fourth lane, where the mammoth was dozing on the northbound curve. He waited for them to finish their workout before approaching them with that joviality that had endeared him to others on the track and told them that a group of runners was being organized in the fourth lane, on Mondays, Wednesdays, and Fridays, from seven to eight in the evening, to run together, which is always better than doing it alone.